The Land
of Lost
Content

The Land
of Lost
Content

ROBERT PHILLIPS

NEW YORK · THE VANGUARD PRESS, INC.

Published simultaneously in Canada by the
Copp Clark Publishing Company, Ltd., Toronto

Manufactured in the United States of America
Designer: Ernst Reichl

Library of Congress Catalog Card Number: 70–134667
Standard Book Number 8149–0674–5

Several of these stories first appeared, in different form, as follows: "In a
Country of Strangers," "Obsession," and "The Quality of Feeling," *The
Carleton Miscellany;* "Songs of Three Seasons," *The New South Quar-
terly;* and "Mealy Marshall and the Whore of Babylon," *Southern
Humanities Review.* Thanks are due to the editors of each of these publi-
cations for permission to reprint. The lines from "A Shropshire Lad"—
Authorized Edition—*The Collected Poems of A. E. Housman,* Copyright
1939, 1940, © 1959 by Holt, Rinehart and Winston, Inc. Copyright ©
1967, 1968 by Robert E. Symons. Reprinted by permission of Holt, Rinehart and Winston, Inc.; Jonathan Cape Ltd., and The Society of Authors
as the literary representatives of the estate of A. E. Housman.

Contents

44845

Into my heart an air that kills
    From yon far country blows:
What are those blue remembered hills,
    What spires, what farms are those?

That is the land of lost content,
    I see it shining plain,
The happy highways where I went
    And cannot come again.

—A. E. Housman,
A Shropshire Lad

FOR MY MOTHER AND FOR MY FATHER

Prologue:
The Happy
Highway

The town of Public Landing is on Route 13, some hundred miles below the old Mason-Dixon line. It is another of those Eastern Shore towns through which the highway runs—another town with the same Main Street as the town before and the town after; the same tombstone-white Methodist churches; the same benches in front of the bank for old folks to sit and hawk upon; the same dreary miles of flat sandy fields and chicken farms separating one town from the other.

Once you have crossed the canal up north, there is little of interest on Route 13, except perhaps for the state's one private college, a junior college long on Jesus and short on funds.

One cannot fail to observe, however, the numerous fudge palaces that dot the landscape: Stuckey's and Horne's and Candy Manor and Peterson's House of Fudge all rear their impressive façades by the roadside. Some of these establishments are man-

sions, really: converted colonial brick mansions with crumbling
white Georgian pillars and new wildly flashing neon signs.
Others are small commercial structures of plastic and steel and
tinted glass, anticipated by omnipresent and mammoth bill-
boards—35 More Miles to Peterson's House of Fudge! 15
More Miles to Peterson's House of Fudge . . . until, finally,
THIS IS IT! PETERSON'S HOUSE OF FUDGE! *The signs are far taller
than the buildings of which they sing.*

Fudge is this country's ruling passion, and the candy stores
are monuments to self-indulgence. In this country gluttony is
mistaken for adequacy. Noticeably lacking on the roadside is the
usual assortment of entertainments—the bowling alleys and skat-
ing rinks, miniature golf courses and dance halls one finds farther
north. Here there is nothing but the homes, the farms, the
chicken houses—and the fudge palaces. The well-to-do amuse
themselves by eating. A day's entertainment is to attend the
groaning board. Scarcely are the breakfast dishes washed before
the men again are raiding the kitchen. Scarcely has the snack
been consumed before the family is clamoring for supper. And
so it goes throughout the day. This is a land in which calories
have never been heard of. To be "healthy" means to be "pleas-
ingly plump," portly, stout; a slender person is looked upon with
suspicion, or pitied and thought to be curiously sickly and
anemic.

With great relish the populace eats slippery dumplings and
corn puddings, hominy grits and sweet-potato biscuits, all accompanied by liberal swigs of Pepsi-Cola, or better, bourbon—even
the prevailing Methodist conscience has not prevented a dis-
turbingly high rate of alcoholism. There is simply nothing else
to do but eat and drink.

For those few youths who have escaped to attend colleges or
take jobs up north, to return home is not to start at the small-
ness of local things, but to be astonished at the local humanity's
size. Overnight everyone appears to have become obese. Family
and friends seem larger than life, bloated beyond reason. But the

high rate of death in middle age goes unnoticed—people here are set in their ways. And their ways are ignorance and gluttony.

Driving down Route 13, the traveler notes the extremes of human existence in this land. One lives either in a gaudy but costly Georgian home set well back from the highway, nestled flatly on bare, sundrenched acres, with pink cast-iron flamingos or black-faced jockeys stuck upon the brown crabgrass; or in a sagging shack hovering directly upon the highway's sandy shoulder. These shacks lean and list, their roofs are tattered tar paper, their windows waxed paper bought in rolls and held fast by thumbtacks. Through their junk-littered yards, anonymous children, nearly naked, chase one another, their voices raised in shrill shouts that sound like glee. But the eyes are stony and dead. You would like to stop, to scoop up an armful of these children, white or black—the poor whites being poorer even than the poorest blacks—and hustle them off to nutrition and comfort. But there is not time to stop on busy Route 13—the tractor trailers full of pullets and melons would run you down. Besides, there are too many children sharing similar needs. Too many. So you take them with you only in your mind's eye, where their expressions send down deep and tenacious roots.

Poverty and wealth sit side by side in ironic juxtaposition: the house trailer that pulled off the road in the middle of the night seems to have camped for years on the plantation's perimeter; the jerry-built shack disgraces the drive where Cadillacs roar and raise dust in finny disdain. Zoning is unheard of here. It is as if the good Lord took a mixture of the very wealthy and the very poor, shook them up, and hurled them down upon this sandy, flat, gray, barren landscape.

By the time you approach the town of Public Landing, you are almost hypnotized by the straightness of the highway and the flatness of the land. Route 13 seems never to turn the slightest degree in either direction, running directly ahead, mile after mile in maddening monotony. You look for, but never see, the fabled Delaware Everglades that lie to the east, those greeny waters with their tall bearded cypresses towering toward the heavens. No, you do not see them, and it is just as well. For man has worked his destruction on those Everglades, reducing them to his own mean level. It was a white man's still that blew up, igniting the cypress forest. No one remembers his name. Yet that one man's mixture of corn liquor and wood-grain alcohol began a fire that raged for eight full years.

To understand how a fire can be so violent, one must understand the geology of that swamp by which the highway passes. Since prehistoric times, gales and tropical storms had felled generations of old trees. New cypresses had grown above the sunken windfalls, which in turn also plunged into the massive ooze and muck of moss and rotting vegetation. Slowly the inextricable swamp closed in and above layer upon layer of the great trees, preserving them perfectly through chemical action. When the swamp caught fire that hapless night, it burned underground even more than above. Accusing fingers of flame reached the great beds of peat that for centuries had accumulated beneath the muck. Sheets of fire burst everywhere, even in the middle of nearby cornfields that had no trees upon them.

Hundreds of volunteers from three counties came to fight the preternatural fire, but it was useless. The fire raged until there was nothing more to burn, until the nymphomaniac fire's insatiable appetite was finally satisfied. Then, with a sigh, it ceased. Eight years of destruction and desolation were consummated. All one could see for miles were blackened stumps.

Today a few lonely old-growth cypress trees remain deep in the heart of what used to be the Everglades and now is merely an overgrown marshland. They stand silent and unpitied, like proud Confederate generals in defeat. They are surrounded only by scrub brush and wild weeds, undergrowth working with deadly copperheads and cotton-mouth water moccasins. Mists rise from the murky warm waters like the ghosts of the vanquished cypresses. A shuddering panorama of buzzards hovers over the stubborn, melancholy wilderness. And so one no longer has even that beauty and diversion.

About four miles to the north of Public Landing there is a religious camp, for those inclined to be upright. It is situated on a dirt road perpendicular to the highway, a road rarely used except for the eight weeks in the summer, when heat and religious fervor are at their apogee. The camp is a large circle of cottages, really—cottages whitewashed and with corrugated tin roofs that the townspeople call "tents," a term that confuses visiting young people, who come expecting great striped canvas tents pitched high on poles, such as one sees in motion pictures about David and Bath-sheba or in illuminated plates of the Books of the Bible.

The camp is the soul of rusticity. There is no indoor plumbing; one relieves oneself in the public four-holer behind the main entrance. Baths, when taken, are endured in rusty pump water, icy cold. The dominant impression, however, is of whiteness: there must be more whitewash consumed at that camp than anywhere else in the world! Even the trees are covered with it, whitely striped halfway up their trunks. The walkways are covered with gold sawdust, and rude benches are scattered here and there between the trees. Dominating the entire vista is the Tabernacle, where services of Christian Witness are held. Open on all four sides—symbolizing, no doubt, the openness of the Four Gospels—with a long sloping roof like a Chinese pagoda, the Tabernacle is a touch of the exotic in the midst of severity.

After leaving the campgrounds behind, one finds the approach to the town rather unremarkable. An illuminated angel tops the True Vine Baptist Church, but that can best be seen after dark, when the greenish-white angel seems to hover phosphorescently in the black sky. That angel on its parapet makes the Baptist Church the tallest structure in Public Landing, the source of rancor for the Methodists. (Once the Human Fly came to Public Landing and wanted to scale the church's façade, clear up to the angel's nimbus, but the Baptists would not hear of it and the Human Fly had to settle for the No-Credit Hardware Store instead, a pitiful wood frame building of only three floors that would have presented little challenge to any man, human fly or no, because the window sills and facings stuck out convenient as ladder rungs.)

Competing in the night sky with the True Vine angel are the lights from Adam Cordrey's illuminated gardens. Adam is an eccentric bachelor whose life work has been to accumulate and decorate his property with thousands of Christmas-tree lights and empty BromoSeltzer bottles. The lights are wrapped around tree trunks and entwined around bean poles that line his many walkways. On top of each pole is an inverted Bromo bottle, its glass bluer than any Baptist window. On several poles are mounted skulls of steers, with red light bulbs planted deep in empty eye sockets. In the middle of the garden reclines a skeleton of a horse, through whose ivory rib cage bloom huge zinnias and swordlike hollyhocks. And over it all, suspended across the central walk, arches a bleached and ancient whalebone. Crudely lettered on each side in bright pink fingernail polish is the legend: A Rib from the Whale That Swallowed Jonah.

In the town other points of interest are the Bijou Theater, with its balcony divided down the middle by a plywood wall, one half for white patrons, one half for black; the Public Landing High School, which has no library but a truly excellent gymnasium; Mrs. Swenson's School of the Musical Arts of the Eastern Shore—nothing but a house, but she once sent a pupil to Juilliard; and the town's two claims to industry, a canning factory managed by a man universally known as Mr. Sam, and, directly up the town's one hill, the Faithful Fertilizer Company. Both flaunt stunted smokestacks in the very face of Whitehall, the mansion of John Hubbard, a former governor of the state who built his home beside the millpond. Until recently Whitehall was inhabited by an extremely old lady and her feeble-minded daughter, Nora Lee. Neither seemed to mind the smokestacks.

Across the pond stands what was the town's third industry, the Sunflower Flour Mill, its building an abandoned and empty shell. There was a time it might have shared the pond with a fourth industry, a giant from the north that once wished to locate in Public Landing. It sent representatives to determine the availability of manpower, to arrange for the acquisition of land, to determine the amount of annual property taxes. But the members of the town council hemmed and hawed. They didn't want to become a prime target for enemy bombs in the case of another war (as it surely would, with industry in the town!). And they didn't want to encourage the possibility of creating a town parking problem. But mostly they didn't want to be invaded by citified strangers—strangers who would come in bringing highfalutin wives and uppity children with peculiar accents and manners.

So the new plant was never built; new schools were never established; new blood never moved in. The town remains spiritually and economically poor. There are fewer people in it today than there were one hundred years ago. But still the wheel on the abandoned mill revolves. As you drive by, you can hear its buckets lumber and creak out of the bilious waters, rattling on and on like some crone repeating ghostly stories to herself. On and on she mumbles, but no one stops to listen. The road passes her by.

Rise Up Singing

Now the Eastern Shore was full of antiquers, but nobody went antiquing with quite the dedication and frequency of Mr. Sam. Nearly every afternoon he would slip away from his downtown office right after lunch, get behind the wheel of his big black Chrysler Imperial, and barrel up and down Route 13 in search of antiques. Sometimes he visited antique shops, other times he dropped in on likely-looking farmhouses and sniffed around. He had been known to drive as far north as New Castle and as far south as Chincoteague. At suppertime he would return home with his prize—another paperweight; another china doll; a piece of gold, silver, or copper lusterware; Chinese ivory or colored pattern glass. With the exception of an old-fashioned melodeon and a big Chinese lacquer screen he once lugged home—a screen studded with figures made of ivory inlay, mother-of-pearl, jade, lapislazuli and

jasper—his taste ran to small, exquisite things. He was a big
man, and his wife, Miss Thelma, was a corpulent woman. Together they would stand in the dining room, before the
crowded corner cupboards, and examine his latest find. They
would handle the delicate object in their pink, meaty hands.
On these occasions Mr. Sam would wear a sweet smile, one of
three expressions he owned: the other two were normal, which
was his look when he was left to himself; and fierce, the look he
adopted whenever anyone mentioned anything about his canning factory.

If he cared to, Mr. Sam could see the stacks of the canning
factory from the side windows of that very dining room. But he
avoided the view whenever possible. The factory was nothing
but a peck of trouble, and there were days when he wished to
God he had never built it, though it was profitable enough.
But even the money couldn't make him forget all the bellyach-
ing that went on over to the factory: the niggers wanting this
and that, indoor plumbing, more up-to-date equipment, he
didn't know what all. Ever since there had been an accident in
the spring, a bad accident, the niggers had been threatening to
strike for better conditions. He wasn't about to spend a cent he
didn't have to on that factory. If the niggers didn't like it, they
knew where they could go. The place gave him a pain in the
ass. The only time he visited there was late at night, after
everyone was gone. He would go under cover of night and let
himself in the high wire gate with one key, and into the factory
proper with another.

"Zat you, Mr. Sam?" old Mose, the night watchman, would
sing out.

"It better be, else you're in real trouble, boy," Mr. Sam would
answer.

The walk between the gate and the factory was what he most
disliked. The place stank. In the summer there were tons of
tomatoes heaped in the yard, a mountain of softly rotting
mush. In the fall the mountain turned to punkins. And they

smelled even worse. There was nothing more stinking than a mess of rotten punkins, Mr. Sam thought. If Mr. Sam could have, he would have avoided the factory altogether. There was always the possibility one of those black bucks was hiding somewhere in the yard with a knife. He had always heard people joke about the proverbial nigger in the woodpile, but only recently had he come to fear just such a nigger might exist. But he kept going to the factory every month or so. Why should he pay good money at the Acme Market for canned tomatoes and punkins and butterbeans when he owned a factory full of them? He would back his car up to the gate on a moonless night and emerge from the factory two or three times, bearing a different carton with each trip. He kept Miss Thelma's pantry lined with cans, and he tried not to think about the knife that might be gleaming somewhere in the dark.

One night in late August, after Mr. Sam had spent an especially satisfying day antiquing in the afternoon and enjoying Miss Thelma's little peas and dumplings and strawberry shortcake in the evening, there commenced a rattling at the back door. Mr. Sam knew it had to be something about the factory; everybody else came to the front door and rang the chimes.

"Jesus God, Thelma," Mr. Sam muttered into his napkin, wiping the remnants of whipped cream off his face. The crushed strawberries had stained his lips bright pink. "Go see who in hell that is." He remained seated at the table, hearing her shuffle across the kitchen floor in her wedgies, hearing her open the door. The sound of crickets filled the kitchen.

"Yes, what is it?" he heard her ask out into the dark stoop beyond.

"Mr. Sam to home?" he heard a nigger ask. Had to be a nigger, with a voice like that.

"He is. What do you want with him?" Miss Thelma always interpreted her role in their marriage as protecting Mr. Sam from outside distractions. A man who worked as hard as Mr. Sam should be able to enjoy peace and quiet in his own home.

"I come to give him a warning."

A warning? Mr. Sam thought. Was this a threat? Was someone actually threatening his life? Had the one with the knife actually come to his very back door? His body went cold and hard as stone where he was slumped in the chair.

"Ask him what his name is, Thelma," he finally managed to say.

"It's just me. Legion Jones."

Legion Jones. It took a while for Mr. Sam to place him, but then he remembered. He was the nigger they had made foreman. Mr. Sam had met him once, as a formality. The nigger had been to normal school for a year, and that had made him uppity even before they'd given him the title of foreman. Nothing worse than an uppity nigger. Just before he had left him that time, Mr. Sam had asked the nigger how he came to get a name like Legion. The nigger had had the good grace to look embarrassed that the question even had to come up. "Well, sir, it was this way," he explained. "When I was born, my mama didn't know what to call me, so she asked for the Bible to leaf through, and she stopped looking when she came to the part where the Blessed Lord declared, 'My name is legion.'"

"If that don't beat all," Mr. Sam had said. "Don't that make you ashamed, boy? That's the most niggerish name I ever did hear." Then Mr. Sam had given the nigger his fierce look, blaring his eyes and staring him into the wall, and said, "Do you think you're worthy to bear a name spoken from the lips of Jesus Christ?"

"I don't think the Lord would mind," the nigger had said.

"How's that?" Mr. Sam had shouted.

"I said, no sir."

"That's better," Mr. Sam had said, and turned on his heel and left, and that was the last he had seen of Legion Jones until this night in August.

"Tell him he can come in," Mr. Sam said, his backbone relaxing with relief. He didn't reckon an educated nigger like Legion Jones (even if that education was only one year of normal school) was likely to stick him with a shiv.

The nigger came in. He didn't have anything in his hands, not even a hat. Mr. Sam thought all niggers wore hats of one kind or other, come evening and putting-on-the-dog time—straw hats or caps with a duck-bill or hand-me-down fedoras. But this nigger was empty-handed and empty-headed. Legion Jones stood in the middle of Mr. Sam's clean kitchen, looking black as tar. He wore clean Sweet-Orr bib overalls with no shirt underneath, just the straps crossing in back and meeting the bib in front. His arms bulged with power. Even relaxed, his biceps were like black tennis balls.

"What's this about a warning?" Mr. Sam demanded, raising himself about an inch from the chair, but no more.

"That's what I'm here about, all right. A warning. The men gonna go on strike next week if certain conditions aren't met. The men got conditions."

"Conditions?" Mr. Sam asked, pumping a tone of incredulousness into the word. "What kind of conditions?"

"I think I'll go along upstairs," Miss Thelma announced. She never could stand to be in the same room with one of those black rascals. Made her uneasy, she said.

"Go!" Mr. Sam said, indicating with the sweep of one huge paw the very door she was to take. "I'll be up myself directly," he sighed, casting his eyes toward the ceiling.

"Now, what kind of conditions you talking about this time, Legion?" he asked, as soon as the swinging door had swung shut behind Miss Thelma.

"Better pay. Shorter hours. New conveyer and pulverizer. Showers for the migrant camp."

The song of the crickets filled the empty space that followed Legion's speech. At last Mr. Sam said, "You must be joshing me, boy. That's it. You come over here to josh Mr. Sam. Ha ha ha."

"No sir, I don't reckon I am."

"A new conveyor belt? What's wrong with the old one?"

"It jams up. Breaks down all the time. Takes five men all afternoon to fix it, and then it ain't right after they do. Just breaks down again. 'N' all the time the cans are piling up and the men is missing work—"

"A new pulverizer?"

"There's been accidents. Just last week a man lost—"

"Showers for the migrants?" Mr. Sam's voice soared. He hoped Miss Thelma could hear him upstairs, to see how firm he could be.

"That's it. That's the ticket. The men reckon you're not about to give them indoor toilets—"

"They're right as rain about that!"

"—so's they figure the least you can do is give 'em showers."

"Showers! If they're getting so persnickety they got to shower, they can get their asses down to the pond and clean up there like some of the white boys do."

"Polluted," Legion said simply.

"How's that?"

"I said it's polluted. The pond. The fertilizer plant been dumpin' chemicals in there for five, six years now."

"Don't talk to me of the fertilizer plant. Don't you think I know what they do and don't do? I'll have you know I'm the biggest single shareholder in that fertilizer plant."

"Yes sir."

"Look at me when you speak, boy. Don't hang your head like that. It ain't at all becoming. Let alone polite."

"Yes sir. Well, I'll be moseying along now. I just thought I'd come and warn you."

"Hold on there. You're not moseying anywhere till you tell me what those black bastards plan to do."

"Do?" Legion Jones looked exasperated. "I done told you. They gonna go on strike. Starting next Monday. If'n you don't promise to meet their conditions."

Mr. Sam thought about that for a few moments. He thought about all the hundreds of thousands of tomatoes that would never get canned and would rot in the sun. And all the tens of thousands of cans that would never get bought. And all the punkins in the ground growing and growing right now, just waiting for fall to come around. "You tell those sons of bitches I'm coming to the plant tomorrow morning at ten o'clock. Tell them to be in the yard at ten o'clock, every man-jack one of them, ready to hear what I have to say. You hear? And tell them I'm bringing the sheriff with me, just in case they got any funny ideas. You get me?"

"I got you."

"And the next time you come to see me, you dress proper," Mr. Sam said, looking at least half-fierce again. "Miss Thelma was so embarrassed she had to leave the room. Don't be coming to a white man's home without a shirt on, you hear? You gotta consider the women's sensibilities."

"I hear you talking, Mr. Sam," Legion said, and then he backed out the screen door, blending completely into the night.

Someone had built a platform out of empty Coca-Cola cases. It stood in the middle of the factory yard, like a politician's rostrum, and Mr. Sam headed directly for it with Lacey Whaley at his heels. Lacey was wearing his badge, the first time Mr. Sam had even seen it. Damn fool's probably as scared of getting a knife in the back as I am, he thought. The day was already settling in hot. Sweat was forming on Mr. Sam's brow. The niggers made way for them as the two of them pushed ahead, the crowd parting just like the Red Sea for Moses. The yard was full of sweating niggers. It smelled even worse than rotten punkins! What is it about niggers? Mr. Sam wondered. He knew they were biologically inferior; that was a proven fact. But what made them smell right brassy?

"Now, you men listen to this," he shouted the minute he had ascended the makeshift wooden platform and put on his most fierce look. "You listen to Mr. Sam. You men got a regular job, eat three square meals a day—am I right or am I wrong?"

For a moment no one answered. Then a voice from the crowd murmured, dry as fodder, "That's right, Mr. Sam." It sounded like Legion Jones, but it could have been any one of them. They all mumbled, every man-jack one of them. It was all he could do to understand them, they talked such mumbly nigger talk. He continued.

"Last year a passel of you voted in the gubernatorial election, and nobody stopped you. Am I right or am I wrong?"

"You is right, Mr. Sam," a voice said, accompanied by some more mumbling and rustling somewhere off in the crowd. Mr. Sam nodded and squinted into the rising sun. His coat already was soaked and sticking to his back. "And I understand, that is to say, I've been led to believe, that beginning this September you can even start taking your children or grandchildren, or whatever it is you've got, to the Public Landing Elementary School. They're going to close down the Booker T. Washington School altogether. A damned shame it seems to me too, a perfectly good building like that, less than a hundred years old. But there you are. That's progress, or what passes for it these days. Is that you-all's understanding? About the school?"

"That's it," a voice said.

"Well, then," Mr. Sam said, throwing out his chest and planting his feet wider on the podium, "if you boys got jobs and regular pay and three squares a day and voting rights and your children—legitimate and illegitimate alike—are sitting *right next to* little white children in the schools, come this September, I ask you—what in hell have you got to complain about?" And before anyone could answer, he rushed on. "Now, you listen to this. You listen to Mr. Sam. The first man who goes on strike in this factory loses his job. And when he loses his job here, he may as well clear out. Yes sir, a man loses his job here and he might as well leave Sussex County altogether, because he ain't a-gonna get another job in the fertilizer plant,

I'll see to that. He's not gonna get a job in the Delmar button factory, 'cause I own that too. And he's certainly not going to get a job at the nylon plant in Seaford, I'll see to that."

He looked around him to see what effect his speech was having. Most of the men were studying their feet with great concentration, as if they were memorizing each hook and lace-hole of their boots.

"And that's not all. There's other things could happen round here. What if—now, I'm just supposing, you understand, don't get me wrong—but *what if* the migrant camp should catch fire some night? My God, what a terrible thing that would be. I hope to God it never happens. But what if it should? Be a terrible thing, boys. All your women and chillun without roofs over their heads. That is, if they got out of it alive. . . ."

Lacey cleared his throat and signaled to Mr. Sam. "Aren't you laying it on a little thick, Sam?" he whispered. Mr. Sam dismissed him with a wave of the hand. "Shut your mouth," he said between clenched teeth. "If anybody knows how to handle niggers, it's me." He cleared his throat and scanned the crowd of blacks before him. They all hung their heads like rag dolls.

There was no strike that summer. There were no knives in Mr. Sam's back, either, just as there were no fires in the migrant camp. As summers in Public Landing go, it ended pretty much the same as any other. But three or four weeks after he talked at the factory, on a day when he had brought home an elegant figure of an Oriental beggar carved exquisitely from one piece of ivory, Mr. Sam was sitting on his front porch, reading the *Southeast Breeze,* when he heard a scream. It was Thelma's scream, coming from somewhere deep in the bowels of the house. He flung the newspaper down and ran into the house, where he found her standing in the middle of the kitchen, her head buried in her hands.

"What is it, love?" he asked, staring at her. Miss Thelma was a graduate of Southern Seminary and was usually the picture of composure, though lately she had been going through something she called The Change, which made her a bit touchy some days.

"I can't look at it. It's just too horrible. I can't look. Take it away."

"For God's sake, Thelma, what is it you're talking about?"

"There! On the counter!"

Mr. Sam looked. All he saw was the can opener, an empty can, and a bowl full of his own stewed tomatoes from the canning factory.

"What's wrong with that?"

"In the bowl," Miss Thelma moaned.

Mr. Sam went up to the bowl and peered in. The finger that floated in the tomatoes had been severed neatly at the joint. There was a gold wedding ring around it, and the flesh was black as sin.

A Lady of
Fashion

"Do you really think I ought to get it frosted?" Thelma said, touching the points of hair protruding from beneath the big flowered beach hat they had insisted she buy at the exclusive import shop on the boardwalk.

"Definitely," said Kenneth. "Absolutely."

Kenneth was the better looking of the two boys, and she usually took stock in what he had to say. It was obvious he knew how to dress, that he had been around ladies of fashion before. The other one, John, was less attractive. He was darker, for one thing, and Thelma had always objected to swarthy men—they somehow never looked clean. John was dark, and his hair was curly to the point of being kinky. The first time she had set eyes on him she wondered if he had nigger blood, but of course that was out of the question. Once he opened his mouth, you knew he was white. He had a simply marvelous personality. His personality made up for the fact that he was so dark and that his eyes were set too close together. Sometimes when you got too near him and he looked at you with those close-set eyes, he looked just like a ferret. But he had a silver tongue in his head, just like Wendell Willkie, and Thelma could sit and listen to him talk all day. Just as she could sit all afternoon on a beach blanket and watch the other one, Kenneth, stretch and twitch and oil himself and sun-bathe until it was time for the three of them to pack up their things and walk through the sand to the boardwalk, where the Purple Pony Cocktail Lounge awaited with air conditioning and gin-and-tonics.

"Kenneth is right, of course. Your hair looks perfectly fine now, but frosted! It would be just too much! It would be the real *you*, Thelma." John rolled the top of his trunks farther down, beyond his navel, to get a more comprehensive tan. He had absolutely no belly at all, Thelma noticed. He was lean and slim as a post. Thelma always had had a tendency toward corpulence, and ever since Mr. Sam, her husband, had died the summer before, she had been conscious of her weight. The first thing she'd done when they told her he had keeled over in the bank and died on the cold marble floor was to reach for a Fig Newton, and she had eaten them all fall, winter, and spring. She had taken to sitting in the front parlor with the shades drawn, eating Fig Newtons all day. She didn't stop eating them until she met these two boys—an act of fate—the day she checked into the Sea Breeze Hotel for the month of July. She had brought three suitcases, two full of clothes and one full of Fig Newtons, because she hadn't known if they sold them at Ocean City and she wanted to be prepared. Then she met Kenneth and John at the Purple Pony and she hadn't set tooth in a cookie since. She figured the Fig Newtons were moldering up there in her hotel room this very minute. Well, let them molder. She saw them for what they were, the Fig Newtons—a substitute for living. When Mr. Sam died, her life

died; despite his shortcomings, she had loved Mr. Sam. He
had always treated her like a lady. Now these boys had taught
her how to live again. She was even becoming more outgoing.
Mr. Sam had been such a dominant personality she had absolutely cowered sometimes.

"Well, I wouldn't want it too light, you know," Thelma
said, twisting a shock of her hair around and around one finger. "I'd look like I'd gone completely gray!" She laughed at
the improbability of such an appearance.

"You wouldn't look gray at all, that's the whole point,"
Kenneth said sharply, as if the matter were closed. "You'd be
an absolute stunner."

The conversation lulled. Thelma took in the scene: the tall
hotel behind her, blindingly white in the afternoon sun; the
sea before her, equally blinding, tossing and turning in its bed
like a tormented sleeper. Camped all about her on blankets
were the other guests of the hotel, most of them impossibly old
and white as paste. She didn't see how some of these women
had the nerve to put on a bathing suit. It was true that she had
put on weight since Mr. Sam died. She had put on quite a
bit, in fact. But at least she wasn't all caved in like some of
these women, their shoulders rounded, their bellies sagging,
their breasts hanging like deflated balloons. These women
looked like all the life had been sucked out of them. They sat
still as stobs on their blankets, most of them hidden from the
sun by large beach umbrellas that Mickey, the beach boy,
planted in the sand every morning. What was the use of coming to the beach if you were going to hide beneath an umbrella
every day? Why, these women would go back to Baltimore, or
Washington, or wherever, just as pale as when they arrived!
They might as well be home in the parlor. They might as well
return to their dark little rooms and rock away another year in
their rocking chairs. As long as she had some figure left, she
was going to take the sun. She was always thankful that she
tanned easily. When the tan came, the freckles did too, but
that was all right. Freckles were healthy. Or were they? Hadn't

she read somewhere just last winter that freckles cause skin
cancer? She shifted her ample behind on the beach blanket as
she tried to remember, frowning in concentration. No, she decided, that couldn't be it. Look at Doris Day. Doris Day and
Van Johnson—both of them were covered with freckles from
head to foot, and she never had heard a word about cancer in
either of them.

Just then a tall woman with shingled hair walked by with a
coolie hat on. It was a pointed coolie hat just like you see in
the moving pictures, and she had on a Hawaiian shirt. Thelma
called it a Hawaiian shirt because that was just what it looked
like to her, a man's sports shirt with a design printed on it in
bright colors, just like Harry Truman used to wear. Thelma
squinted into the sun and finally could see that the repeated
design was of a man standing in a little boat, catching a big
blue fish at the end of the rod. The fish leaped out of the water
and had a big round eye. It took some time for Thelma to make
out this design, because it had been printed upside down all
over the shirt. Now, why would anyone make a shirt like that,
she wondered, with the design upside down? Better yet, why
would anyone wear it? And that hat? She wouldn't be caught
dead in a hat like that. It all went to show that money can't
buy taste. She had said it a hundred times before, and here was
living proof. It cost a lot of money to stay in a hotel like the
Sea Breeze, yet this woman walked around looking like a
clown.

"Shall we head for the Pony?" John asked languidly, and
they began to gather their things. Kenneth stopped to talk to
the blond beach boy as they made their way through the sand.
John talked with Thelma very loudly, waving his hands before
him. Thelma felt the eyes of the other ladies upon them. Well,
let them look, the old coots. They didn't still have their figures. They didn't have anything interesting to talk about with
young men the way she did. She could thank the blessed memory of her father for the education he had given her. He had
sent her to Southern Seminary and had seen to it that she re-

ceived the education of a true Southern lady. She had learned elocution and the history of art and rhythm of dance and just everything. Why, in her senior year she had even been queen of the May Fete. Which of these ladies glaring at her could say the same?

"So I said to him, 'You think I'm just another one of these fool tourists, don't you? If you think I don't know the difference between real delft and that fake Japanese stuff you're trying to sell, you've got another thought coming—'" John continued, his close-set eyes rolling like a pair of dice. Snake eyes, Thelma thought. Then he stopped and glared back at Kenneth and Mickey talking by the umbrella stand. In the late afternoon sun the beach boy was a series of triangles: his eye sockets were two triangles, his nose one, his shoulder blades another pair, his thick pectoral muscles two more, and his crotch the last. All the while they talked, John's little ferret eyes kept darting back to Kenneth and the boy. Finally Kenneth left, giving the beach boy a playful push and running toward Thelma and John. When he reached them he wasn't panting at all, though he had run hard and the sand was deep. In such good shape, Thelma observed. And he's not really a boy any longer. He's had his own dress shop for ten years.

"He'll come," Kenneth said to John. John smiled.

"Come where? To the Pony? They won't let him in. They're very strict about minors," Thelma said.

"No, this is for later. John and I felt kind of sorry for poor Mickey, working hard like that all day. We thought we'd take him to the movies or something tonight. That is, if it's all right if we use your car?"

"I've never minded before, have I?" Thelma said, leaning on the railing by the boardwalk steps and putting on her sandals. "You know I like you boys to have a good time."

The following morning Thelma had an early breakfast in the hotel dining room. Kenneth and John were not yet up, so she took a single by the window and ate more rapidly than usual. She had gone to bed early, since the boys had elected to treat Mickey to a movie, but she had not been able to get to sleep. She missed what had become their routine these past several weeks, the three of them having dinner together at one of the smart restaurants at the north end of the boardwalk, then going to a night club where they danced. The boys took turns as her partner. They hung on her every word; she told them about the life she used to lead with Mr. Sam when he was alive, and they were fascinated. She told them all about the book circle she belonged to and the ceramic class she used to attend. She told them about her house full of antiques. She even told them about her orgy of Fig Newtons and they had laughed with her. Then the boys would go off in the car when she retired.

As she lay awake during the night, she had listened to the carnival-like noises coming from below her window on the boardwalk. She had listened to the sexual slap of the sea on the shore. And to the organ music coming from the Sea Breeze Cocktail Lounge. The organist played "An Affair to Remember," "La Vie en Rose," and "Fascination," three of her favorite songs. She lay with her hair trussed up in curlers and a mud pack caking and cracking on her face, and thought how wonderful her vacation had turned out to be. She had expected to come here and end up sitting on the porch rocking like an old biddie. Instead she had been rejuvenated by young talk, young thinking, young actions.

Thelma got up from the breakfast table and made her way down the porch toward the parking lot and hairdresser's. She didn't have an appointment but she reckoned she didn't need one this early in the morning. Who has her hair done at nine in the morning at the beach? Nobody, that's who, she figured, and she was right. Miss Doreen was able to take her immediately, and by eleven-thirty Thelma's hair was heavily frosted, just as the boys had insisted it be. As she walked back to the car, she felt at least twenty years younger and as many pounds lighter. Her sandals barely touched the pavement.

It was after she returned the car to the hotel parking lot that she found them. She had parked the black Chrysler and was ready to sail into the lobby, looking for the boys, when she remembered to look for the earring she had lost the Sunday before. She had worn her good pearl earrings to the morning service at Our Lady of the Sand Dunes and she hadn't seen one of them since. She had intended to look for it in the car before, but the boys had used it every night since. She opened the back door and began to feel beneath the front seat. Before she knew what it was she had, she had pulled them out. Standing in the parking lot, she straightened up, holding a pair of soiled jockey shorts in her hand. There was a faint smear of shit inside them and they reeked of rutting men. She knew that smell. It was the smell of Mr. Sam after he had finished heaving and grunting on top of her. Sometimes she had felt that man would split her wide open, pulling and hauling the way he did. Anyhow, that was the smell, and it was on these underpants. She dropped them to the soft asphalt beneath her feet and walked back into the hotel. She did not look further for the earring.

"I swear, but you look just like Miss Jean Harlow in 'Red Dust,'" Kenneth said when she settled herself on the beach blanket that afternoon, her hair a creation of silver and platinum and gray.

"No, no, not Harlow at all," John protested. "Let me think who . . . Miss Bette Davis in 'Of Human Bondage'? No, that's not quite right either, though she was blonde as hell in that flick."

"How about Dietrich in 'Golden Earrings'?" Kenneth offered.

Thelma didn't say anything, just shifting her weight from ham to ham and listening to the two of them go on. She noticed that Mickey was back at his umbrella stand, conducting business as usual. She couldn't see that he had been harmed any, but you never could tell.

"Well, whichever, you look just too, too divine," John said, exaggerating his syllables in a way that made Thelma smile despite herself. What, after all, had she expected? The jockey shorts in the Chrysler had only been an outward sign of what she already knew. It was obvious what these boys were. All her life she had heard about boys like them, but she had never known any. They existed on the margins of her experience, boys like Robin—what was his name? Robin Winslow, the boy who used to traipse all over East Street in his mother's high heels and dresses the minute she lay down for a nap. And he only eight or nine years old at the time. The shame of it! And Brendon Bailey, the janitor out at the Public Landing High School. The one that was so sick in the head. They caught him doing something or other to one of the junior-high-school boys right in the broom closet.

No, Thelma was not surprised at what she had found. But she was disappointed. Kenneth and John were such smart young men. They knew just how to handle everything, from the snooty *maitre d'* at the Chinese restaurant down the board-walk to one of those tricky surfing boards. How could young men of such taste, such cultivation, such accomplishment, get themselves involved in anything so . . . so sordid? Surely those were Mickey's shorts in the back of her car. Kenneth and John would never wear underwear like that. They'd wear silk boxer shorts, cut full with a balloon seat, like Mr. Sam used to wear. She was sure of that.

"We thought we'd use the car again tonight, Thelma. That is, if you don't mind?" John was saying.

"You'll do nothing of the kind," she snapped. "You'll take me to the Ship Cafe Inn and this time *you'll* pay for the lob-sters," she said with satisfaction. "From now on you're paying your own way."

"Hey—what kind of talk is that?" Kenneth said, raising his rectangular-shaped sunglasses as if to see her better.

"You heard me," she said firmly. "And the car's to stay in the lot for the duration."

"Well, I'll be damned. What's the matter, Thelma? You wearing the rag or something?"

"As if she'd have to," John snickered.

Thelma chose to ignore that last remark. She plunged on. "Look, boys, I know what you've been using my car for. I didn't say anything the first couple of weeks, when you were running around with that Chico or Pancho or whatever that spick waiter's name was. He was old enough to look out for himself. But Mickey, he's something else. He's still a kid, and I won't aid and abet the corrupting of a minor. After all, I have my positon to consider. I'm a lady, a graduate of one of the finest colleges in the South. . . ."

"You're an ignorant bitch and an insufferable old douche bag," Kenneth said, his handsome mouth pulled down in an ugly line.

"The most insufferable old douche bag I think I ever did encounter," John added. "I don't know how we've even stood the sight of you all these days, those folds of fat, your crooked teeth, and that hair!"

"My God, yes, that hair! It *really* looks like a rat's nest now, doesn't it?" Kenneth shrieked. "It's every color of the rainbow!"

"And then some," John said, tittering.

Thelma sucked in her breath for a moment and listened to the sound of the sea. She sat hugely on her beach blanket while the two of them looked at her—a big ugly woman with a ridiculous straw hat upon her head, a hat with four bobbing orange cabbage roses. She had on too much rouge and she looked just like a clown. Her hair was streaked severely and cut in a style thirty years too young for her. In her legs the varicose veins showed like blue twine. Finally she pulled herself up, dragged the blanket behind her, and went to her shaded little room. She lowered herself into the one chair, opened the suitcase of Fig Newtons, and began to eat.

Mealy Marshall and the Whore of Babylon

Black as a telephone and twice as talkative, Mealy was the oldest and darkest human I had ever seen. She was expecting us when my father stopped the car before that listing shanty she and her brother called home, and she came out on the porch before we could even honk the horn. She latched the front door with a long key, dropped the key into the bosom of her dress, and came down the steps to the car with some sort of satchel on her arm.

As she clambered into the back seat my father turned around and said, "You don't have to ride in back."

She blinked and then said consideringly, "Well, suh, I'm here now, so ah just reckon ah'll stay put." She laughed a nervous little laugh, then turned her gaze upon me where I sat beside my father. Her eyes were a special warm brown with white flecks—exactly like my favorite agate marble that I had refused to trade with any boys up north where we used to live, and for which I'd already had three elaborate offers from newly made friends in Public Landing. I studied those eyes, so bright in that ancient dark face, and her heavy lips, so purple they could have been stained with grape juice.

As we drove across town toward home, I sneaked glances behind me to the satchel she had dragged into the car. It was a tired and dusty-looking reticule that I supposed contained all the belongings she cared to bring. Mealy was to be our live-in maid, to look after Billy and me and to do all the things Mother couldn't do because of her crippledness. My father insisted on paying Mealy exactly what he had had to pay our maid in New Jersey, which must have made her the best-paid Negro in Sussex County.

After she had been with us a few months, we realized the salary meant nothing to Mealy. Her husband was dead, her children had gone off long ago, and her brother worked regularly at the cannery. So every Friday when Father paid her, she folded up the bills in her red bandanna and stuffed it in that reticule. It might have been string she was saving for an enormous yarn ball she would someday unwind. All my mother's persuasions could not convince Mealy she should take her money to a bank. She went to the bank for us—cashing a check for Mother, depositing a check for Father—but she never conducted any transactions of her own.

We all loved Mealy immediately, and she returned our love, but in disparate amounts. She was fully devoted to Mother— always trying to make her more comfortable, pushing her wheel chair from the shade to the sun, the sun to the shade. She gave Father respect, honesty, and a fair return for his money. Toward me she was congenial but cautious, as if a trifle afraid of what I was going to say or do next. But to my older brother Billy she gave a love that grew and grew like a crazy sweet-potato vine. At the end of a day she would pat me on the head, quickly tuck me in for the night, and then rush into Billy's room. She would sit for hours on the side of his bed, telling him wild superstitious country stories, or rubbing his back and shoulder blades that were sore from junior-varsity football. Sometimes Billy tried to trade stories with her, but you could tell he was making them up as he went along. His stories were usually pointless and stupid, and I could never understand why she laughed at them. But laugh she did.

I still don't know why Mealy had such a preference for Billy. He wasn't as bright as I, not as good in school. And not nearly so talkative. Perhaps it was because she could tell I was my mother's favorite. Perhaps this was an expression of Mealy's sense of justice, balancing the scales between Billy and me. Or perhaps memory gives Mealy too much credit. She may have preferred Billy because he was so much better looking than I. All his life he was known as "the handsome one"; I was "the bright one." I should have much preferred it the other way around. I already had been jealous of my brother's handsome face, his thick curly hair. (I was hollow-cheeked and my hair was fine and straight as corn silk.) Then when Mealy came to stay, I had further cause for jealousy. But I think now that Mealy did not mean to slight me, to be undemocratic or unchristian. Her heart favored Billy, and she followed her heart. He was simply her favorite, and there was nothing she would not do for him.

Mealy Marshall was an anomaly in Public Landing. Besides "living in," an unheard-of situation in the town, besides cashing checks for a white man in the First National Bank, she was also the first Negro to drive a white man's car. When my father had been transferred, he became supervisor of the local branch of the Faithful Fertilizer Company. He spent long hours at the plant, my mother was confined to her wheel chair, and so it was Mealy Marshall who drove us to school, shopped for groceries at the supermarket, and ran errands all over town. She was called, often to her face, "the Davidsons' nigger." Parking our beat-up Chevrolet at the curb, she would enter a store in

time to see a storeowner wink at a customer and say, "God
help us all. Here comes the Davidsons' nigger!" And the customer would most likely remark that it appeared Mealy never
seemed to shut up, morning, noon, or night.

I have to admit Mealy was a talker. My mother used to joke
that her own infirmity would be easier to bear had it been
coupled with deafness: "Here I am, bound to a chair, and I
can't turn you off!" she joked to Mealy. Mealy would look at
her with concern troubling those agate eyes, and solicitously
ask, "You want Mealy to shut up? Ah'll shut up iffen you
wants me to." And my mother would say, No, of course not,
she was only joking—at which Mealy would continue her jab-
bering, rattling the Venetian blinds she was dusting in furious
accompaniment. When Mealy dusted the blinds, you could
hear the clamor throughout the house. My father was exposed
to Mealy's banter less than half the time the rest of us were,
but he told her one day he was going to take her up to Washington.

"Washington Dee-Cee?" she asked in disbelief. "What for
you want to take me to Washington Dee-Cee?"

"To register you with the Patent Office. I read somewhere
there's no such thing as a perpetual-motion machine, and I
want to show them they're wrong!"

Mealy laughed and laughed at that little joke, and over the
years she occasionally would stop in the middle of one of her
endless tirades and say, "Ah'll be dad-blamed iffen ah don't
sound jest like Mister Davidson's Perpet'ral Motion Machine!"

I loved to hear Mealy talk. When my mother and father
grew weary of her chatter, when Billy ordered her out of his
room in disgust because he was trying to build a model car or
listen to the radio, I would seek her out and provide an audience for her prattle—in that husky Southern voice I found a
security I've never felt before or since. But Mealy would never
stay by my side too long. If Billy didn't wish to hear her story,
the story must not be worth the telling, and she would return
to her housework or retire to her room.

As Billy and I grew older, the gulf between Mealy and me grew wider. When I entered junior high school, I began to realize my potential as a student. As soon as school was out, I'd come home, lock myself in my room, and study for hours. Billy never came home after school. He always had football, basketball, or baseball practice. He would not get home until after seven o'clock. Mealy would save his dinner and heat it up for him. Then the two of them would sit at the kitchen table and lose themselves in a world of their own. Billy would tell her all about practice, and how he was becoming the best player on the team. Mealy would tell him everything that had happened during her day, the accidents with the laundry, the stubbornness of the vacuum cleaner. And sometimes Billy would help her with her speech. Mealy had decided that more than anything in the world, she wanted to learn to talk like a Northerner. She would make Billy repeat words and she would try to pronounce them the same way. If she made a mistake, she would laugh her high, other-worldly laugh and Billy would boom out as manly a laugh as possible. His voice was a long time changing, and he had little control over its range.

Sitting in my room over the kitchen, I would hear them in concert, and I felt empty as a china cup. I could have helped Mealy with her elocution lessons ever so much better. My voice wasn't changing yet; I talked on pitch all the time. And I could have taught her words Billy didn't know. He never read books. Yet by the time I was in high school, even under Billy's inexpert tulelage, Mealy had dropped some of her Southern inflections, a change that was noted about the town and further confirmed suspicions of her "uppityness."

Once my mother asked Mealy if she wasn't proud of my studying so hard. I sat waiting some word of praise, but Mealy shook her head. "It's selfish study, that is. Bucky studies all the time so he can bring home a good report card, so you'll fall all over him, near about. Anybody studies jest for praise, why, that's selfish! But Billy, now, that's somethin' else agin. Billy doesn't study so's he can talk to ol' Mealy! Somebody got to talk to her, and Billy elected himself. That's *un*selfish, Miz Davidson."

We all knew, of course, that Billy would do anything to avoid homework, and Mealy was a convenience. It was assumed he would never go to college: his grades were shameful. But toward the end of his senior year the coach got him a scholarship to play football at the state university. Then Billy talked of nothing else the entire summer. I looked forward to his leaving.

Father had a meeting at the plant the day Billy was to go away, so it was Mealy who drove him the ninety miles to the university, making Billy Davidson the only college freshman to move into his dormitory under the personal and undivided supervision of his nanny. That must have presented some spectacle for the other students: my brother, by that time a tall and heavily muscled athlete, kowtowing to that ancient, incessantly talking Negress as they delivered his suitcases, trunk, sports equipment, and other paraphernalia to his room. Mealy told me they hugged each other and blubbered like babies when it was time for her to leave. I'm sure it was so.

After he went away, Billy sometimes wrote letters addressed to the family, and occasionally he wrote letters to Mealy alone. Whenever she got a personal one, Mealy would scuttle off to her room, throw herself on the bed, and read it over and over again. She kept all Billy's letters in a yellowed cigar box, and on evenings when her work was done she would spread them out all over the bed and study them like Scripture. Billy wrote he was doing very well on the football team. Apparently this was so: he sent a clipping from a city newspaper that showed him in uniform with the caption, "The Cannonball Express." Mealy didn't know why anyone would want to call Billy a cannonball express, until my father explained it referred to his speed. "His speed on the football field," I said sarcastically, "not his speed in the classroom."

In another letter, Billy mentioned he had taken up golf in

gym class and was enjoying the sport. The afternoon of the day
that letter arrived, Mealy extracted a fistful of bills from her
red bandanna and borrowed the car to drive downtown where
she bought the finest set of golf clubs at the No-Credit Hardware Store. She brought them home, hauled the gleaming
leather bag into the house and up two flights of stairs, and
propped it in a corner of her room. The clubs were her Christmas present for Billy.

Then Billy didn't get home at Christmas. The football team
received a bid to play in a bowl on New Year's Day, and he
spent all vacation in practice sessions in Miami. Mealy didn't
see how anyone could play inside a bowl, until my father pa-
tiently explained what a stadium looked like. Then Mealy
told everyone she saw on the streets that Billy Davidson of
Public Landing was going to be on television. Soon most of the
town had plans to watch the game—except us. We didn't own
a television, and Mealy knew they wouldn't let her in the bar
at the town hotel because she was colored. For a time it looked
as if she wouldn't get to see the game, and she moped around
the house for days, saying even the Christmas tree looked sad
and sickly this year. Finally a neighbor invited our family over
to watch on their set, and Mother insisted Mealy be invited as
well. She sat apart from the two families, perched on a stool at
the other end of the room, but she never took her eyes off the
screen the full two hours. "Is that him? Is that one our Billy?
What number is he got anyhow?"

But Billy didn't play. He warmed the bench with the other
freshmen. "Where's my Billy?" Mealy hollered at the television
set when the game was nearly over. "Put in Billy boy!" She was
positive if the coach had sent in her Billy the school would not
have lost the game, despite a final score of 72 to 0.

So Christmas came and went, and the golf clubs remained in
the corner of Mealy's bedroom. In time the red satin ribbon
around the bag drooped, but Mealy kept the clubs dusted and
shining. She would give the present to Billy when he came

home in the spring. Billy wrote Mother he was coming over Easter, and that he was bringing someone from a neighboring town with him: a girl with the preposterous name of Sue Hornblower.

"What kind of name is that?" I wisecracked at the dinner table. "Hornblower! Is she any relation to Captain Horatio? I'll bet she's some beaut!"

"Try not to form preconceived notions of a person just on the basis of a name, would you please?" my mother said emphatically. Actually, she was troubled over the prospect of Billy's arrival with a girl. His grades had been disastrous the first semester. She and Father had planned to have a long talk with him. They were going to try to persuade the Cannonball Express to give up his athletic scholarship, to quit sports and start studying before it was too late. But now that Billy was bringing home a girl, matters were complicated. There might be no time to have their talk after all. Mother was anxious not to interfere with Billy's plans, especially where a girl was concerned. Despite his good looks, Billy had had little to do with girls in high school, preferring to herd around with the boys on the teams.

"He didn't write me nothing 'bout no Hornblower," Mealy complained after the letter arrived. "He writes me 'bout everything important, and he didn't mention no Hornblower. She can't amount to much," Mealy concluded, lovingly wiping off the gift putter with a cheesecloth rag.

"Gee, I don't know, Mealy," I teased, knowing whatever I said would be taken to heart. "Maybe he's finally found himself someone he likes better than you."

"Well, then, that be all right. My Billy goin' to find himself a nice white lady someday. That's jest nat'ral. Only this isn't the girl, or he would have told me 'bout her."

The morning Billy arrived was cool and clear, a day when daffodils swayed on the lawn and blue jays screamed behind the house in the woods. It was a Saturday, and I was raking up soggy wet leaves on the front lawn, a job I didn't much relish, when I heard a racing motor. I looked up and saw a sparkling yellow convertible pulling in the drive. I thought it was the handsomest car I had ever seen—white-wall tires, wire wheels, racing stripe, the works—and Billy was climbing out of it! On the driver's side a petite girl with long red hair slammed the door behind her. It closed with a solid thud.

"How's Mom?" Billy asked the first thing, and then he introduced me to Sue. She was not as beautiful as I had imagined she might be, but she was pretty enough to make me feel adolescent pangs of envy and desire. I was now a high-school junior, and occasionally looked up from behind my textbooks to notice the blossoming girls around me. They never returned my stares. Now Sue Hornblower stood before me, a full-grown woman with a powerful car. She must be full-grown, I remember thinking, because she used so much make-up. Her eyes were outlined in black, her lips were blood red, and she wore a little half-moon of sapphire blue grease on each eyelid. She looked like my conception of a movie star. Her voice was very light and very, very Southern. When she clattered up the sidewalk in transparent plastic, high-heeled shoes, I followed like a puppy. I thought she was wonderful. I cursed Billy and his good looks and easy ways.

"Where's Mealy?" Billy boomed into the hallway. His voice had long since found its natural timbre, and now he manipulated it proudly. "Where's my Mealy Marshall?" Mealy came clip-clopping down the stairs in her mules faster than I had ever seen her run. She had a feather duster in her hand, but she threw both arms around Billy and kissed him resoundingly on the cheek. Sue began peering into her compact mirror.

"Is dat really you?" Mealy asked joyously. "You really come home to old Mealy?"

My mother wheeled her chair through the living room and out into the hall. I think she was startled by Sue's exotic appearance, but she was, as always, gracious. She took Sue's hand

and they began making small talk about the drive downstate.

"Come on up yonder," Mealy urged Billy through it all. "I got somethin' for you—"

Mother stayed behind because of her chair, but Sue and Billy and Mealy and I formed a small procession up the stairs to the second floor and then up the second flight of stairs to Mealy's room.

When Billy saw the clubs, his jaw dropped open in surprise. I stood by silently: Mealy had given me a dictionary for Christmas, and it had cost about one-twentieth what those clubs cost. Billy threw his arms around Mealy's scraggly old neck and was thanking her all over the place when Sue spoke for the first time since we entered the room.

"Billy, ah smell nigra."

"What?" Billy asked in astonishment.

"Ah said ah smell nigra, honey. You know. Ah've never *been* in a nigra's room before. Ah never knew it smelled . . . you know . . . so *different.*"

There was silence in the room. Sue stood there, her delicate little nose twitching, and I wanted to strike her down dead. But that was Billy's job. And he didn't do anything at all, except to say a few words to try to pass it over.

"Don't be silly, Sue," Billy said, trying to sound playful. "There's no smell in this room, nothing except incense or maybe that special lemon soap Mealy's so crazy about. I'll bet that's what you mean. Pine incense and lemon soap."

"It's not pine or lemon ah smell, Billy. It's *nigra.* Ah know it is. Ah've smelled it in buses before. It's enough to make a body sick. Ah'm going out for some air. Ah'll get my bag from the Buick. Then ah want to wash up. My poor stomach's about to turn over from this smell!"

Mealy didn't say anything at all. She merely lowered herself heavily upon the bed like a sack of grain, and sat mutely staring up at Billy's hesitant face. Her hands were in her lap, turned upward, and the palms were smooth and light and wrinkled as the lining of an old pair of shoes.

After Sue left on those transparent heels that looked like icicles, I sat down on the bed next to Mealy. "She doesn't know what she's talking about," I said. "She's just a Southern girl. There are girls like that out at the high school. They say awful dumb things. They say the colored janitor looks like a monkey. They say he's just two generations out of the jungle—"

"Hush you mouth, boy," Mealy snapped at me. Then she spoke to Billy, who was carefully inserting his new golf clubs one by one in their handsome bag. "What you let her talk to old Mealy like that for?" she asked softly. The voice quavered.

Billy took his time with the clubs. "Aw, gee, Mealy. She didn't mean it. She's just funny about certain things."

"What you let her talk like that to me for?" she repeated, demanding an answer.

"Because I love her, I guess, Mealy," was my brother's reply.

Mealy tightened the line of her flaccid lips and looked him square in the face. "She look like a painted Jezebel to me. She all got up like the Whore of Babylon—"

Billy impatiently shoved the golf bag into the corner. "That's just the style, Mealy. You don't know what's going on out there in the world. All the girls wear make-up like that nowadays. That doesn't mean anything."

Mealy stared out the one narrow window of her attic room. The sun was climbing higher in the sky. Soon it would be noon.

"You gonna marry that girl, Billy? You gonna make her you wife?" Now the voice was drained of all emotion, a mere husk of a voice.

"Yes. I think so. If she'll have me."

"That's all Mealy want to know."

When my father came home for lunch, the meal was ready. Mealy had cooked a huge ham the night before, and it had been importantly decorated with pineapple rings and cherries and displayed atop the kitchen counter all morning. When Father came home, it was as if a signal had been sounded: Mother wheeled her chair into the dining room, Father took his place at the head of the table, and Billy and Sue sat on the far side, holding hands under the lace tablecloth and laughing foolishly. I hesitated in the archway. Out the window I could see her obscene-looking yellow car squatting toadlike in our drive. I had no appetite. I didn't want to sit at the table with Billy and Sue.

"Sit down, Bucky," my father said impatiently, making up my mind for me. He was anxious to return to the plant. He was so preoccupied with work, he had had very little to say to Billy and Sue in the living room.

I pulled out the chair across from Billy and sat down. As soon as my napkin was unfolded, Mealy popped her head through the swinging door dividing the room from the kitchen and said in a voice I did not know, "Y'all ready now?" The inflection was exaggerated as one in a minstrel show.

"You can serve any time, Mealy," Mother said, looking up questioningly.

"Oh goody, *good good.* It's all nice and pipin' hot, jest the way ah knows y'all likes it! MMMM-*mmm.*" She elaborately smacked her lips. Then the grizzled old head disappeared into the kitchen.

"Here it comes, yas-sir," she enthused, bursting through the door with the ham on a platter surrounded by glazed potatoes.

"Mistah Billy, you gets de furst slice, 'cause you is de guest ob honor! De guest ob honor ob dis house!" Her eyes rolled up into the top of her head. "You is de one and de only Cannonball Express!

" 'N' Miss Suzanne, honey, you gets de *second* slice! It's not ever day we has a charmin' lady come to call!" From deep within her came a comical old cackle as she passed the ham around the table. Then she stood there, cackling for a moment, and shuffled back toward the kitchen. She lingered in the doorway.

I looked at Billy for his reaction, but he simply sat there

holding Sue Hornblower's hand and staring at his plate. His usual empty smile had not been altered.

"If deres anythin' y'all needs, jest give old Mealy a call," she chuckled, and then, before exiting through the swinging door, she turned and gave Sue Hornblower a long, considered smile of welcome. Then she disappeared. She may as well have tied her red bandanna around her head.

I wanted to leap up and fly into the kitchen, to grab her by her bony neck and squeeze and squeeze until those rolling eyeballs and grinning teeth popped from her head like Chiclets. I wanted to squeeze this hideous caricature, this Aunt Jemima, until the real Mealy Marshall returned. But the door had swung shut and my family was beginning to eat. So I picked up my fork and began.

Obsession

In the fall of his twenty-eighth year, Fooks took to writing directly to Chambers of Commerce. Prior to that—he thought—the obsession had kept within bounds. It was a source of disturbance, surely, but fortunately, it had touched the outer corridors of his life only dimly; for a bank teller, appearances were all. But one evening—it was a hot September evening, as a matter of fact, and he thought he could hear cicada chirping on West 95th Street, as ridiculous as *that* was—he said out loud in the silence of his cluttered room, *The hell with it!,* got the address of the Public Landing Chamber of Commerce from one of the travel folders he had hoarded in his littered room, and wrote them.

"Gentlemen," he wrote, "I want to know all about the South. Tell me what it is like. For too long now I have been shielded from its beauties and its terrors alike; now in the gray drain of my lost adolescence, I wish to know details, facts: What is the annual precipitation? What is the state of the soy-bean market? Are the girls homey or are they promiscuous? Can you still buy marshmallow Moon Pies for a nickel? Tell me, gentlemen; tell me and if you state it well, I may move my small industry to Public Landing and join you in perpetuity."

It was a good letter. He read it, checking for errors of spelling and punctuation. The next morning he mailed it Special Delivery on the way to the bank. In due course he got a reply, but it was only a set of folders with pictures. A form letter was enclosed with a box checked: WE CANNOT COMPLY WITH THE DETAILS OF YOUR REQUEST. So that was that. But you might as well be hanged for a sheep as a lamb, so Fooks wrote Richmond the next night and the night after that he wrote Salisbury and eventually he wrote Biloxi, careful to specify, however, that he was not interested in getting involved in the racial situation. Folders came in in abundance but none of them was satisfying.

It was just too much. That was all—it was too much. And then he realized that the Chambers of Commerce had nudged him over a line: he was in a dim whitened space, a space of enlarged possibilities. *The obsession enacted is the obsession retracted,* he said to himself—and about that time he got fired from his job without notice and with two weeks' severance pay. They told him that his work had fallen below par; that his distracted manner was demoralizing everyone in the bank. Fooks knew that conditions had coalesced. It was time to go South. Not to think about the South, study about the South, even dream about the South, but actually to *go* there.

Because he had read all of Faulkner (and all the other Southern novelists too, for whatever good it did him when he tried to work on his own book) he said "Oxford" when the ticket agent asked him his destination. He had taken a subway to the Port Authority Terminal to reserve his seat the night before he planned to go. He was afraid if he waited until the

morning to buy his ticket, there might not be any room left on
the bus and he would lose his nerve and never come back to
the terminal again. He got his ticket to Oxford and put it in
his pocket. It occurred to him to wrap it within a knot in his
handkerchief, as he had read old mammies do with their coins
for safekeeping, but he dismissed the notion immediately and
began walking up Eighth Avenue. The city screamed around
him. A siren caterwauled into the night. Soot fell from the sky.
But for the first time in more months than he could remember,
Nathan Fooks felt an inner calm: this time tomorrow night he
would know.

It was still early evening. He felt the luxury of time on his
hands. His bus did not leave for fifteen more hours. For want
of something to do, Fooks wandered into a delicatessen and,
after a five-minute wait, repeated the question that over the
months he had asked in hundreds of West Side delicatessens:
Do you sell collard greens? (The novels in his bookcase at-
tested to truckloads of collards consumed in the South, and
months ago Fooks decided that if he could eat just one good
mess of collards—Southerners always spoke of vegetables in
terms of "messes," that much he knew—his memory would be
aided. One taste of collards—how *did* they taste: sweet? sour?
gritty? bitter?—would instantaneously trip a floodgate of
memories of the several brief but supremely happy years he
had spent in the South as a young child before his family
moved to New York City to live beneath the rumbling shadow
of the Third Avenue El. He had read Proust's statement that
all of *Remembrance of Things Past* had been evoked by one
taste of a Madeline dipped in tea; surely one taste of collards
would be enough to enable him to write one slender volume?

So Fooks stood there in the Eighth Avenue delicatessen,
amidst the acrid odors of belly lox and creamed pickled her-
ring, and once more inquired after collards.

"Collard greens!" the middle-aged Jew behind the counter
shouted at him, wildly gesticulating. "Collard greens the man
wants! So what are you, some kind of a nut?" The Jew's cheeks

were blue with heavy beard stubble, and his face became red with outrage. "How many collard greens you think I would sell if I stocked them?"

Fooks had been subjected to this kind of vituperation by storeowners before (it must be something in his manner of asking, he thought), but each time he never knew what to say. Other customers always stared at him, and usually he ended up backing out of the delicatessen in embarrassment. But this time, as he blinked nervously under the store's bright fluorescent lights, he felt a playful tug on his coat sleeve. He wheeled around and the girl was standing there. Her dress was white and youthful, the skirt was stiffly starched. She looked like the Queen of the May. Her long hair fell straight to her shoulders and was almost the color of Christmas tinsel.

"What y'all want with *collards?*" she asked cutely, wrinkling her little pink nose like a rabbit. "Don't you know nobody eats collards but nigras and po' white trash?"

Fooks glanced about the store to see if any Negroes were present to have been offended. Then he relaxed and confronted the girl. He smiled.

"Say. Where'd you pick up that accent, huh? You from the South?"

"Why, *however* did you guess!" she teased, and laughed a wonderful laugh, a laugh light, rippling, and metallic, like someone upsetting a stack of new dimes. Her laugh made the short hairs on the back of Fooks's neck prickle. There had been a girl in his Sunday school who laughed just like that. Now Fooks listened to this girl's laugh and realized that here, on the eve of his odyssey, he had found what he was searching for: she was from the South. Of the South. Had lived there all her life, judging from the thickness of the accent.

"I thought I had become Northern-ized, but I suppose I still sound pretty Southern." She heaved a little sigh of resignation.

"It's a beautiful accent. Don't ever lose it." His hands were perspiring profusely.

"You really like it?"

"It's beautiful," he repeated, realizing he sounded foolish.

She smiled and walked away on little pink plastic heels. The delicatessen had emptied now and the proprietor elaborately drummed his fingers upon the cash register in impatience. The girl set her carton of eggs and container of milk on the counter. The blue-bearded Jew added two figures, the cash register rang. The milk and eggs were bagged. If Fooks didn't say something, she would walk out the door, to disappear forever into the caverns of the city.

"Look," he said anxiously, "can't we talk some more? I've got some time. I'd love to talk some more. About you. About the South."

Her eyebrows were black but her hair was silver. Her hair glinted in the cold artificial light and she said softly, "Well . . . I happen to know a little place right around the corner. I live over it upstairs, so it's sort of my hangout, don't you know? If you'd be so kind as to carry my bag like a true gentleman, we could go there and have us something nice and cool to drink."

Fooks was not much of a drinker, but he said quickly, "I'd like that! Juleps? Do you ever drink juleps?"

She made a little face. "Those sweet things? Mercy, no! And whatever were you looking for *collards* for?"

She laughed that laugh again, and her silver bracelets jangled like little Oriental bells. Where had he heard a sound like that? On old Dick. His grandfather's draft horse. Whenever his grandfather gave the harness a jerk. Fooks had been afraid of old Dick (who must have been the most docile and stupid of creatures), afraid because the horse was so huge and smelled so bad and because as a boy he was so little and tried to keep so clean for his mother. The girl's bracelets jangled again as she swept past him through the door he held for her, and she said over her shoulder, "In case you're wondering, my name is Bonnie Rae."

The bar was dark and dirty, with strips of flypaper hanging

from the ceiling, globbed with dead insects looking like raisins, but for once Fooks didn't mind such things. Just so they could talk, nothing else mattered. Bonnie Rae chose a small table in the corner and he held her chair while she settled herself prettily. His whole body trembled as he sat opposite her. They almost had the place to themselves. Two sad fairies sat at the bar, and an old henna-haired woman with a stomach as big as Asia pretended to watch the television.

"You don't suppose they have Dr. Peppers here?" Fooks asked Bonnie Rae.

"Dr. Pepper? You crazy or something?"

"No." He stared down at his big moist hands resting on the table top and then quickly withdrew them, hiding them in his lap. "I just thought for sure you'd like a Dr. Pepper, if they have them. Didn't you drink it when you were a kid?"

"We had big R. C. Colas and little Grapettes, but we never had Dr. Pepper!"

"Well, you missed something. Gee, when I was little, Gramps and I used to go down to Maddie's Confectionery for Dr. Peppers, and all the colored folks who worked in the cannery would be there having their lunch. And that's what they'd have, too: Dr. Peppers and a package of Lorna Doones . . . I remembered that, just the other night." His voice trailed off.

"I'm not no nigra and I didn't come here to drink *soft* drinks," she said. "Aren't you going to buy me a martini?"

"Sure. Say, you didn't ever go to Sunday school at the True Vine Baptist Church in Public Landing, Delaware, did you?"

"I should say not. My daddy's the *Methodist* district superintendent! Besides, I never set foot in Delaware, 'less you count riding through on the bus when I left Savannah to come up here. I never even considered that the South. . . ."

"Oh, it is—just like the South, only you have to live there to know it." Then he added, "You sure sound like a girl in the True Vine Sunday school. You laugh just like her."

"I'm not her."

"No, of course not. I guess Southern girls all have a special way of laughing. I just haven't heard it in so long."

"That must be it." She smiled and cast her eyes about the room.

"I wish I could remember the hymn we used to sing. It was pretty and we used to sing it nearly every Sunday. But I can't ever recall it."

"You will. Now, how 'bout that martini?"

Her third martini looked as cold and lethal as the first, somehow reminding Fooks of formaldehyde. He nursed a mug of beer and kept asking things he had to know.

"What did those trees look like? The cypresses you mentioned?" His fists clasped and unclasped beneath the table.

"Lordly, I've *told* you pret' near all I know." Bonnie Rae laughed.

"Please . . . the cypresses?"

"Oh, all right. But I'd think a body would get sick and tired of hearing all this after a while. There's nothing so great about the South, believe you me. Or else I wouldn't never have come all the way to New York City!"

She sipped the cocktail and looked at him over the rim of the long-stemmed glass. "Let me see. Well, they were in a big swamp. There was this great big old cypress swamp on the edge of town. Huge old trees just *covered* with Spanish moss that hung down and trailed into the water just like a woman washing her hair! And there were lots of knobby cypress knees that jutted up out of the water. Ninepins we called them, 'cause that's what they looked like—"

Nathan was furiously taking mental notes.

"Look, what do you want to know all this junk for anyhow?"

"A book. I'm trying to write a novel. About the Eastern

Shore—. What it's like to grow up down there . . . it was the only time in my life I've ever been happy."

"Well, Christ, it's *your* childhood. You don't need to hear any more of this palaver from *me*."

He wanted to cry out, *But I do need to hear it, I do. Because I can't remember, I can't think for myself any more. . . .*

She fished in her purse for a quarter and then walked over to the ancient nickelodeon. He heard the coin drop in, the sound of three buttons being pushed one by one. The nickelodeon flashed all the colors of the rainbow, but the colors were faded, tired, washed out and used up.

"You like to dance? They let you dance in here. That's why I like the place." She was standing beside the table, her silver hair glinting the rainbow colors.

"I can't dance. Come on, sit back down."

"That's all I do, dance. I'm a professional dancer." She sat down obediently.

"You teach at Arthur Murray or something?"

"I could show Arthur Murray steps would make his wig spin! Naw, I don't mess with that ballroom crap. I'm a tap dancer. At least, I am when they let me be." Her long white finger toyed with the olive in the bottom of her empty glass.

"When *who* lets you?"

"You know. Casting directors. Producers. Anybody. Nobody *wants* a tap dancer in New York City! Oh, they tap-dance back home all right. You just go by Madame LeCheval's living room of a Saturday afternoon and you'll hear her students tap-tap-tapping their little hearts out, pret' near. But not in New York City. No siree. I go to an audition and tell them I'm a tap dancer and they like to laugh their fool heads off. They do! They laugh right in my face. Because nobody up here tap-dances any more. I might just as well specialize in the soft-shoe or cakewalk."

The silver-haired girl looked sad and Nathan Fooks reached out and stroked her tresses with his big clumsy hand.

"It's all right," he said, though he didn't know if it ever would be. Things were different in the South from anywhere else, he was sure of that. The apotheosis of tap dancing just served to prove it.

She reached up and touched his hand where it stroked her hair. She patted it lightly and said, "You know, you're nice. Real nice. I hope you get that book written."

"It'll get written. It has to. It's all I want to do."

"Well, you can't write it tonight, so why not forget about it, huh? Just for tonight? You'll burn your brains out, thinking about it so much. Listen, I have some beer in the 'frig upstairs. If you don't want to dance, there's no need of staying here—"

She twitched her nose again. Where had he seen a nose twitch like that before? On the farm. A scared rabbit he once chased through the tiger lilies. Was it an Easter present, that pink-eyed rabbit? Or something wild? When it held its ears erect, you could see the light shining through, the skin was so delicate and thin. With little red veins tracing through like markings on a road map. He wanted to hug the rabbit but it ran through the yard full of sassafras bushes and scurried into the bed of tiger lilies. Behind the shingled house and the rusty pump that sounded like an old man's cough. Sassafras bushes have three different kinds of leaves. All on the same bush. Sometimes even on the same stem. Some of the leaves look like mittens. Mitten leaves, he called them, though no one else did. The harness jangled and the Sunday-school girl laughed and the little rabbit nose twitched. Where was that rabbit now? With old Dick. Three kinds of leaves. Good to chew on. Bitter but sweet. Wanted to love the rabbit.

"I don't want to go upstairs," he said. "I want to sit here and listen to you. You might not talk upstairs. You wouldn't have your music." His hand fluttered toward the nickelodeon like a crazed bird.

"You don't want to dance, you don't want to drink, all you want to do is *talk, talk, talk!*" she screamed over the music. Two sailors just settling themselves at the bar turned to look.

"The obsession enacted is the obsession retracted," Fooks said softly. His eyes were closed and he seemed to repeat the words by rote.

"Huh? Listen, mister, you're talking awful funny. You sure you feel all right?"

He opened his eyes. The sailors were looking at him. He realized he hadn't eaten all day and his head was beginning to reel. "Where's the men's room? I've got a call of nature."

She pointed and he lurched out of his chair and started in that direction. The floor seemed to buckle beneath him and he barely reached the toilet before he began heaving up his sour sorrows. After some time he flushed it, studying the whirlpool in the bowl.

Then he splashed cold water on his face and dried off with a paper towel. He combed his hair and made a note to ask her about sorghum. There were things about sorghum juice and slippery dumplings he had to know. If only he had more time, he could unravel it all, could remember what it was he had to know, and why he had to know those things. He pushed through the swinging door and walked toward the table.

It was empty.

He turned to the bartender to ask if she had gone to the ladies' room and then he saw that the two sailors were gone too. The bartender shrugged his shoulders and smiled a crooked smile. Fooks began to feel dizzy again and the floor resumed its buckling beneath his feet. He paid the tab to the bartender, who kept smiling, and walked out into the mad street. He located the door to the apartments above the bar and entered the narrow hallway. Panting like an animal, his back wet with perspiration, he climbed the steep wooden stairs. Paint was peeling and flaking from the walls, and a single naked light bulb dangling on its wire illuminated the landing.

As Fooks walked down the tunnel-like hallway he heard her laugh. He stopped before the door and listened to her laugh and to the two male voices intermingling with hers. Then he knocked softly. The laughter and the talking broke off then, seemingly suspended like a question mark in the air. He knocked again.

(Now he remembered the hymn they sang in Sunday school! "Rescue the perishing, care for the dying . . ." The windows were all open and the air was clear and sweet and they raised their reedy voices to the rafters. His mother would come for him after Sunday school and they would go for ice cream together while his father still slept.)

Fooks waited several minutes and then found himself listening for her breathing. She was in there but she was pretending she wasn't. She was hiding from him. It was a game. (They played hide-and-go-seek and he always hid in the hayloft, but Tommy Sudcliffe always found him wherever it was he had buried himself beneath the dusty hay. Fooks was always afraid that in looking for him Tommy would stab into the hay with the pitchfork, but he never did. The pitchfork was like the bayonet Fooks had to use and keep clean in the Army. The pitchfork and the bayonet glinted and were sharp and they scared him with their cold efficiency. If Tommy used the pitchfork to find him, it would go right through his thigh or his neck and yet it was supposed to be only a game. Why must someone always get hurt in games?)

Now it was not a game. He knocked on the door again, harder this time.

"Bonnie Rae? Bonnie Rae, let me in. It's me. Nathan." As he said it, he realized he had not even told her his name. He knew hers but she didn't know his. So he quickly added, "The man who bought your drinks."

Silence.

"Please, Bonnie Rae."

He heard the bolt slide on the other side of the door. It slid efficiently into its groove and he realized again how fiercely he hated bolts and bayonets and anything mechanical.

Then he heard the rustle of her white Sunday-school dress and he held his breath.

"Go away," she whispered through the door. Then all was silent again, as if the words had never been uttered.

"Let me in, Bonnie Rae!" he screamed. Something had happened to his voice; it was different now. He pummeled his fists wildly against the door. *"Don't lock me out!* Don't!" He leaned against the door and began to cry in the dim hallway.

The door opened a few inches. She pressed her head to the crack, safe behind the chain that still held fast, and she said, "Go away. You're sick."

Her face was flushed and he saw the flash of some red undergarment she was wearing. He saw the dark at the very follicles of her hair, and she crossed her arms over her small hard breasts as if to protect herself, as if the stout chain securing the door were not protection enough.

"You've got to let me in!" he roared, but the door closed in his face with terrible finality. Screaming, he slid down the door and crouched before it, clawing at the wood with his nails.

The Lost Child

Whenever Nora Lee lost herself in the boxwood maze, she would call out to her mother, who would come to find her.

For fifty-five years Nora Lee had been losing herself in the simple puzzles of that maze, and Regina Hubbard always retrieved her. Regina would be sitting at embroidery, or sewing scraps of lace, or reading through rimless spectacles, when the plaintive cry of her lost child would come from the end of the back lawn. She would hurry out the back door and down the leaning wooden steps to find her. It was a blessing, of course, that Regina Hubbard at eighty-some years of age still possessed all her faculties; her eye and her ear were sharp still. To any octogenarian this would be a blessing. To Regina Hubbard it was especially so: Nora Lee was a half-wit. She had been born that way, and all her life she had been protected by her mother.

Bringing up Nora Lee had not been easy. When she was born, her father, John Wilcox Hubbard, was governor of the state, a brilliant man in his prime. He had tried to hide the fact of Nora Lee's handicap from the public, but of course she was found out. Official visitors to their home and gentlemen from the newspapers always wanted to see the Governor with his family. Nora Lee was the only child, and had to be paraded forth, her eyes glazed, her head slightly too big for her frail shoulders.

Now a widow all these many years—John Hubbard had died young; he was bright, but burned out like a candle—Regina dreaded the thought of what would become of Nora Lee when she died. Distant relatives and townspeople had always hinted that Nora Lee actually belonged in a "home." They would send her to Farnhurst, an institution up north for the feeble-minded. Regina had not had an easy time keeping Nora Lee at home.

The two of them played games. Each afternoon Regina would ask Nora Lee to fix her tea. That was one of the things Nora Lee had learned to do. She would fuss about in the kitchen for an interminable time, then finally emerge into the living room, bumbling about with the tarnished tea tray, the amber liquid sloshing over cup rims and into china saucers. But each day she prepared the tea, and when there was money for cookies, they had cookies, soggy from spilled tea, and they sipped together sitting in the window seat overlooking the sloping, weed-riddled front lawn. Regina would tell Nora Lee that no one made tea as well as she, and Nora Lee would smile a broad crooked smile of satisfaction and twist at the red birthstone ring on her right hand. And every day Regina had Nora Lee make her own bed. The daughter did not relish this job, and pretended sometimes to forget. When that happened, Regina would lead Nora Lee into the bedroom like a naughty schoolgirl, and stand with her bony arms folded until Nora Lee had tidied the sheets and smoothed the rose chenille spread as she was instructed. There were days when she seemed unable to arrange the bed in any semblance of order. When that happened, great tears would spill down her cheeks and Regina would finish the job for her.

They lived in a beautiful old house just across the bridge on the outskirts of Public Landing. The home had once been a plantation, with acres of land on every side. Its six white pillars extended up for three stories, bigger around than a fat man's girth. It had been the handsomest house in the town, and it had been the home of a governor; visitors to the town would seek it out as a site of interest. They would make a point of seeing Governor Hubbard's mansion and Adam Cordrey's illuminated gardens. But the local people tended to avoid the Hubbard house. Miss Regina and Miss Nora Lee were thought to be "different." Everyone knew Nora Lee was "not right," that she should be put away. Children were told not to play near the house for fear some unspeakable evil might befall them. Indeed, the two ladies of Whitehall, as the house had been called for generations, did present a singular appearance. Regina, nearly six feet tall, with snow-white hair, a raspy voice, and old-fashioned clothes, was a vestige of some long-forgotten time. Nora Lee, her hair pepper and salt, bedecked herself in all manner of garb. Because she was very short and often wore her mother's dresses, her skirts dragged the ground. Her clothes always smelled unclean. Children hurried past Whitehall, terrified that one of the old ladies lurking behind the shutters might grab them.

There was a time when the Hubbards were well-fixed financially. Then John Hubbard's heart attack wrenched him away, leaving the two alone in the great old house. Regina had had the education of a true Southern lady: she knew no practical skill or trade whatever. She could only entertain prettily and embroider with considerable detail. Nora Lee, of course, had had no suitors, and there would be none. Regina did the best she could. The servants were let go, and after a period of years

Regina had to start selling off the land. The property to the east, across the street, went first. She sold it to Mr. Sam Fletcher, who said he wanted to build a fine home there. Three weeks later construction began on the canning factory that to this day is a blot upon the town. The factory was jerry-built from sheets of metal and scraps of lumber. A long row of tenement shacks for migrant workers was thrown up beside the factory, and these soon were overspilling with boisterous Negroes and their many children. Regina once remarked that it appeared as if slave quarters had returned to Whitehall after all. She was upset about the factory, but not so much so as the townspeople who lived farther from it. There were some who never forgave her the factory and the Negro workers it brought to Public Landing. They never blamed Mr. Sam; they pointed the finger at her. The air was continually filled with the rumbling of cans jerking down the conveyor belt, and the grounds in front of the factory were filled with mountains of softly rotting tomatoes in the summer, pumpkins in the fall. No one but poor white trash in the town would purchase anything canned there, the factory's filth was so discernible. The neat little cans of tomatoes and pumpkins were shipped up north, to Philadelphia and beyond.

The property to the north of Whitehall was sold a number of years after the factory was built, and on that land were erected a neat dozen development homes. The homes all looked alike, but they were moderately attractive and young couples of moderate means moved into them. Later still, Regina sold a little postage stamp of a piece of land across the street from the factory where Maddy's confectionery store was opened. Its dealings were primarily credit transactions with the migrants, and providing odds and ends like bread and sugar that the housewives in the development forgot while shopping in the town at Junior Collins' grocery store. Regina retained the front lawn down to the road, and the back yard all the way to the little stream that gurgled there, a tributary of the millpond behind the factory. Her front lawn blossomed with forsythia, magnolia, and japonica each spring. The box-wood maze in the back yard had grown tall, very tall, until Regina no longer could peer over the top. She would sell no more of her land.

Inside, the house had grown shabby. The velvet antiques were slick and bald from the bottoms of countless Hubbards and Wilcoxes through the years, the rugs were worn thin, and the floor boards creaked wherever you walked. The entire effect, however, would still have been one of charm had it not been for Nora Lee's eccentricity. Nora Lee loved to arrange the furniture, and she had it in her mind that all the chairs should be against one wall, all the floor lamps against another, the tables against still another. Regina had ceased trying to rear-range the disorder Nora Lee created: her daughter always tugged the furniture back to where she wanted it as soon as Regina left the room.

Nora Lee had two other activities that consumed her inter-est. One was listening to the radio; the other was playing in the sandbox of one of the little girls in the development. Nora Lee would sit with her ear pressed against the dim tubes of the ancient radio, listening with great concentration to afternoon soap operas. Then she would trudge out onto the lawn and wander over to the development where she would fall heavily into Susie Pusey's sandbox, spending hours shoveling pure white sand into the small blue tin pail she found there. Mrs. Pusey always chased her away whenever she was home, yelling "Loony, Loony, stay away! We don't want you here!" Some-times she came after Nora Lee brandishing a broom. But Nora Lee always returned whenever the thought of the sandbox came to her, and she would play until Mrs. Pusey appeared. When Nora Lee arrived and fat little Susie was in the sandbox, the blue-eyed girl would scream with fright and indignation and run away before Nora Lee had barely settled herself in the sandbox, a crooked smile pasted on her face.

Tic-Tic Bodine stood outside the main door of the factory and wiped sweat from his narrow forehead. It was hot. It was August and the summer had been a long one. Tic-Tic had made more money this summer than any other season in his life. Tomatoes had been good, there had been enough rain, and he had worked overtime every night for six weeks. But he was broke. He couldn't win at dice this year and every Friday after Legion Jones distributed the pay envelopes Tic-Tic rolled dice. All the men played and now he owed most of them money. He couldn't stop playing—if he did, they would press him to pay up in full what he owed to each of them, and he couldn't do that. He paid out what he could every Friday, just barely saving enough to buy milk and cereal for Estella and the three children. Estella was pregnant again and said she had to drink a lot of milk. Tic-Tic stood before the rattling factory in the white heat of August and tried to add in his head all the amounts he owed. He tried to remember all the IOU notes he had signed, little bits of paper with his mark on them, and his head reeled.

Tic-Tic wiped his damp meaty hands on his jeans and walked away from the factory, out the wire gate that separated the canning factory from the road, and headed across the street to the confectionery store. He had a dime in his pocket and would buy a Dr. Pepper or a Grapette or perhaps a Royal Crown Cola. It was hot and a soft drink would help him think. Everywhere he went there was someone holding out his hand for money to be repaid, and he had to think what he was going to do. He couldn't get in another fight. One more fight and he would lose his job for sure. Maybe he would leave Public Landing suddenly, in the middle of the night. But Estella would not be able to go. They would have to walk and the children were small and she was hugely pregnant. Estella didn't even seem to have enough energy to get out of bed these days. She would never make it to the northern part of the state, where he thought about going and forgetting all his debts.

Boy, would they be surprised when he was just gone one morning. Maybe he would leave Estella and the kids behind. They would get along.

The Grapette was cold and the sweet drink made his teeth ache. He gulped it quickly and was putting the empty pop bottle in the wooden case on the sawdust-covered floor when Susie Pusey came in. She was seven years old, with yellow ringlets, and she was dressed up for a birthday party to be held across town later that day. Her starched pink dotted-swiss dress rustled when she walked. Black patent-leather Mary Janes glistened on her feet as she minced toward the soft-drink cooler. Tic-Tic studied her pink and gold prettiness and spat on the floor. Susie looked cutely at Mr. Clapham who owned the store and asked for a Nehi orange. She stood there until Mr. Clapham lifted the heavy lid off the cooler and pulled a tall orange bottle dripping from the water. He opened it with a snap and passed the fizzing bottle to her tiny outstretched hand. She set the bottle on the counter and zipped open her flowered purse. The purse jingled with coins, silver and copper jangling together. She fished out a nickel with two plump fingers and presented it carefully to Mr. Clapham. Then she quickly zipped the purse tight and carried her soda out to the front of the store, where she sat on the weathered bench and sipped slowly in the shade of the tin eaves. Her mother always had told her that if there were nigras in the store, she should take her drink outside. She had not given Tic-Tic a second look, but she knew what to do.

Spitting again into the sawdust, Tic-Tic watched Susie through the store window, her fluffy dress spread out carefully over her legs, the patent-leather shoes gleaming in the sun. She held the flowered purse tightly in her fat little fist. Tic-Tic's mind was racing: who could tell how much money was in that purse? Fifty cents? A dollar? Those clothes sure cost something. She was rich. He knew which house she lived in, and her daddy drove a big Buick automobile. There might even be enough money in there to pay off something of what he owed. Or enough for a bus ticket to somewhere.

Tic-Tic waited until Susie finished her drink. She left the bottle sitting on the bench and merely walked away, toward the house. He hesitated a minute and then started after her, walking slowly, deliberately retracing her steps in the dust. She didn't look back or seem to hear him behind her. When she got to the street that led to the development, she turned right instead of left, and headed toward the millpond behind the factory. Tic-Tic smiled as she entered the line of trees near the pond. It would be easy to take the purse from her back there. No one was around, and sounds of machinery and conveyor belts in the cannery were so loud no one would hear her if she cried out. Susie sat on the rocky bank near the water line and started tossing pebbles idly into the pond one by one. She didn't see Tic-Tic until he was standing beside her. She saw the heavy work shoes, his black toes protruding through ragged holes. She smelled the sweat of all summer's labors soaked into those stiff clothes. And she looked up quickly with a little look of annoyance on her chubby face.

She wouldn't let go of the purse. She held onto it tightly and he had to grab hold of her arm to twist it. He twisted and she screamed a high-pitched scream and he put his hand over her mouth even though he knew no one would hear. She kicked at him and he hit her across the head and that was when she fell back into the water, not far out, but just at the edge. She fell into the water and her head struck one of the big rocks jutting there. Her head struck, not making much of a sound at all, but cracking like an egg, and then she floated at the scummy pond's edge.

The purse had landed on the bank and Tic-Tic scooped it up and stuffed it into his pants pocket. It was his lucky day; if she had carried it into the water with her, the purse would have sunk straight to the bottom like a stone. Suddenly he felt scared. He looked about him and then lit out into the trees behind the dam, away from the full pink skirt spread out upon the water's surface like a huge water lily.

Nora Lee was bored. It had rained the night before and the sand in the sandbox was damp. It stuck to her elbows and knees and felt gritty. She heaved herself out of the sandbox and looked for something else to do. She had not made her bed and was afraid to go back into the house just yet. She wandered down the street, out of the development, and started toward the pond. There had been a bull frog there the last time it rained, and it made a funny sound. The frog had gone *gerump! gerump!* and Nora Lee had laughed and laughed.

Gingerly she walked about the stony bank, cocking her head every so often in hopes of hearing the frog. Her head was cocked and she was concentrating with all her main when she saw out in the water, being carried slowly by the drift of the dam, the pink dress and yellow hair of Susie Pusey. Nora Lee knitted her brow severely and wrung her liver-spotted hands together for several minutes. Then she waded out, up to her thick thighs in the cold water, until she could reach and grab the purpling arm that was Susie. She dragged the body to the rocks and propped it sitting upright like a doll, the long curls dangling like snakes. Then she ran breathlessly down the road toward the house that owned the sandbox, wet shoes squishing obscenely on the asphalt.

Mrs. Pusey was in the yard, her hands on her hips, calling out to Susie to come home. She would be late for Patsy's birthday party if she didn't come home immediately. Mrs. Pusey's voice was as shrill as Susie's, and she was in the midst of a high, piercing yell of *"Sooooo-Sieeeee"* when Nora Lee came crashing through the bushes that separated the Pusey lawn from the next. Nora Lee was panting like a dog in summer, and her long black jersey dress was torn and slapping wetly against her heavy thighs as she moved. She was wet and muddy from the waist down, and Mrs. Pusey was revolted by the sight of her.

"Loony," she cried automatically, "go away. You can't play here. This here is private property. It don't belong to you folks no longer. . . ."

Nora Lee now was standing directly before Mrs. Pusey, a musky smell about her, like the smell of the old buffalo in the Wilmington zoo that Mrs. Pusey once had seen before she was married. "It's *your* little girl, Mrs. Pusey. She's *yours*," she heard Nora Lee saying in her singsong voice.

"She's not here. She's off buying sweets, most likely. Now, you go home."

"Your little girl. Over there." Nora Lee looked pleased at having some special news.

"Where? Where is she? You've seen her?"

"She's pretty. But she won't let me play with her in the sandbox. She cries too much."

"Where did you see her?"

"At the pond. Over there." Nora Lee tossed her head in the direction of the pond.

"She couldn't be. She would have heard me calling her. Susie *always* comes when she is called."

"At the pond. I left her. Hair got all wet," Nora Lee mumbled, confused that Mrs. Pusey wasn't pleased with her news. A little bit of slobber driveled down Nora Lee's chin.

"Her *what?* Her hair? What did you do to her, you loony?"

"She fell in. The water. Now I can play in her sandbox all the time."

"Good *God!*" Mrs. Pusey moaned, racing around the side of the house and darting across the road toward the line of trees and the millpond. "Sweet Jesus, sweet Jesus."

Nora Lee again settled herself down in the sandbox, smiling beatifically, and this time she didn't seem to mind the dampness of the sand. She closed her eyes and rested in the box.

Regina too was looking for her daughter. Her black cat had followed her out to the front porch, the two of them forming a stately procession, and they stood there together on the portico between two of the six white pillars and her eyes scanned the horizon. Her eyes investigated the factory grounds, the road leading to the pond, the street through the development, and Mr. Sam and Miss Thelma's home. She stood there until her thin legs ached so she had to return to the living room and seat herself in the tapestried rocker. The cat leaped into her lap and nuzzled his orb-shaped head into her scraggly bosom. It was past teatime and Nora Lee had not come home. Even on days when she had been naughty and not made her bed, she came home before now. She usually tired out long before four o'clock and noisily returned through the back door.

Regina rocked to pass the time and when the knocker on the front door was slammed twice she stopped in midrock and sat suspended in space and held her breath until the knocker struck once more, its sounds reverberating through the house, up the staircase, and into the hollow chambers overhead. It was the sound Regina had dreaded ever since Nora Lee had been born. She steeled herself and rigidly walked to the door and opened it to let Mr. Pusey in.

The rest is legend in the town. Nora Lee, of course, had fought with Susie Pusey—there were marks and scratches on the little girl's arm—and finally had hit her in the head with a rock. Everyone knew that Nora Lee should never have been allowed to wander around loose all these years. She had even pushed the girl's body into the pond and then pulled it out again, as if it were a sailboat or some sort of toy. Mrs. Pusey said her daughter always had been terrified of the loony because Nora Lee was jealous of her sandbox. "Her *sand*box, for God's sake," Mrs. Pusey had screamed to visitors expressing sympathy.

Mr. Pusey managed to find a good lawyer from the city, but still he couldn't get any money out of Regina Hubbard. There was no money to be had. Besides, the daughter had never been in her right mind and was not responsible for her actions. Mrs.

Pusey would not rest until Nora Lee had been committed, not to Farnhurst just up north, but to a hospital for the criminally insane in Pennsylvania. In her later years Corinne Pusey derived some cold comfort from the knowledge that at least she had had the loony put where she belonged once and for all. Mr. Pusey chopped up the sandbox for kindling wood, and they lived out their days alone together in their development house that peeled paint regularly every three years, the cellar continually seeping water.

Regina Hubbard's mind failed rapidly after they took Nora Lee away. A big white car had come on a day late in August and in fifteen minutes' time Nora Lee was gone, out of her life forever. Regina felt new miseries in her bones, and it seemed in the weeks to come she could not see so well. She had a bad cough that she could not shake. One morning in early winter she could not sleep and she heard Nora Lee's voice calling to her for help. Nora Lee was lost in the maze again. Regina grabbed her woolen shawl and tugged it about her sagging shoulders. The wind whipped through her thin nightgown when she stepped out into the yard, walking on grasses stiff and hoary from morning frost. She entered the maze and the voice grew louder and more desperate, but she couldn't find Nora Lee anywhere. Finally she realized Nora Lee must have gotten out; she was outside the maze and Regina was wandering within. She tried to find the path that took her to the outermost circle of boxwood but it escaped her. Every turn she took was wrong; she always found herself back in the center of the maze where she had begun. Cold twigs grazed her face sharply as she sought a path in the dim morning light. Her legs ached beneath her. She tugged the inadequate shawl closer to her frame, and with a whimper she realized she was hopelessly lost.

The Kill-Joy

His name was Righteous Fellows. All the terrible puns we students could have made on his name occur to me now, when we are older and sufficiently learned to apprehend his name's connotations. But to us it was just another name: There was Mick and Terry and Peter and Billy (me), and there was Righteous. Certainly if I had been clever enough to see his name as more than name, to realize its irony, I would have snickered as only seven-year-olds can snicker. Because he was the most unrighteous boy in school. Loud, braggardly, bullyish—who could describe him? But sometimes even now, at night, as I lie abed, I see his youthful face—unchanged, unaging, not like mine—floating greenly across my bedroom wall.

He was several years older than the other boys in my class, and he had a tough face. Whereas mine was round and marshmallow pudgy, his was long and hard. He had what I have

since learned to call a lantern jaw, an
the cleft in his remarkable chin: deep,
like a hole bored by a brace and bit. My h
soft as slugs; his, pink as boiled shrimp an
farmwork. I remember the back of his neck, re
pigskin; it was etched with a half-dozen lines tha
like tire tracks rutting a muddy road. His body wa
lean, so long-waisted that all his shirttails spilled
blond hair was stiff and wiry, not soft like mine. He se
young man, though he could not have been more than nine or
ten. When he laughed, which was not often—he was too busy
scowling at the town boys like me—you could see that one of
his two big front teeth was a dull bluish-black. Dead, he said.
He had got in a fight with his older brother, who socked his
jaw so hard it killed the nerve. Righteous seemed proud of it,
though I would have died of shame. The sock didn't even
loosen the tooth, he said. Just made it turn color. It was the
color of a mussel shell. And I always associate the smell of to-
bacco with Righteous—strong, something like Luckies or Cam-
els (we were living in the pre-mentholated era then)—so he
must have at least carried cigarettes, if not smoked them.

He carried other things as well. His pockets seemed an endless source of the unspeakable. One day he brought a baby
garter snake to school and left it in the teacher's top desk
drawer when she left the room for supplies. He knew she always kept her attendance book there. He knew she would open
the drawer after recess and reach in. He knew, he knew. And
one day he brought to school a half dozen Fuck Books. That is
what he called them. They were about two-by-four inches in
size, stapled at one end.

Now, the word "fuck" sounded miraculous to me. I had become a collector of words, exotic words like "muck" and
"Zulu" and "scrimshaw" and "platypus" and "potentate" and
"Zanzibar." "Fuck" seemed to fit into this category. But at
recess, when Righteous pulled me off to a corner of the play-

and showed me the books, I saw they were not exotic or ...ating at all. They were just comic books showing my favorite funny-paper characters like Blondie and Dagwood, Superman and Lois Lane, all doing peculiar things to one another on some enormous sofa or on the floor. And the man in each book, whether it was Dagwood or Superman, always had a wee-wee that looked as big as a baseball bat. I didn't want to look at the books, they weren't even drawn well: even I could see that this Blondie and Dagwood didn't really look just right, not like the real Blondie and Dagwood at all—their faces were somehow wrong, and the lines were all scriggly. I tore myself away from Righteous Fellows and his Fuck Books and ran into the school, where I hid in the toilet stall until recess was over. Once Piggy Harrington came and rattled the metal door; he wanted in, but I continued to sit with my pants down to my ankles, pretending I was there on business. After Piggy went away—making a funny groaning noise, I guess he really had had to go bad—I inspected my wee-wee and thought it looked hopelessly small. Compared to Superman's in those books of Righteous's, mine was hardly there at all. I sat and wondered how many years it would take before my wee-wee grew big as a baseball bat.

It seemed to me then that Righteous devoted his waking hours to tormenting me. It is understandable now why he chose me—a dentist's son, living in town in a white house with geraniums in all the window boxes, dressing in corduroy knickers that went swish-swish whenever I took a step, spending most of my recesses reading or painting with poster paints inside the deserted classroom while the others tore up and down the playground. I was a hothouse plant, pampered, sheltered, taking what sun I took behind dusty glass. So Righteous was wickedly inventive: he dropped toads and snails down my shirt front and watched me dance in terror. He held me down and rubbed my face in the biting snow. He snipped all the buttons off my mackinaw. Periodically he wedged me into the dark supply closet and from the jar forced handfuls of thick, sticky white Milton Bradley paste down my throat. I must have eaten a gallon during the course of one school year. He would knuckle my forehead with nubbins until my brains ached. But worst of all, he desecrated my art.

I had been executing a long mural on brown Kraft paper that was taped the full length of the back blackboard. My subject was St. George and the Dragon. Even now I can see that mural, the huge white horse with its gorgeous tail and mane pluming in the breeze, handsome St. George full-panoplied astride the steed. The only aspect of the painting that gave me trouble was the dragon. I had only seen a dragon once, in an illustrated storybook, and my retention of its shape was somewhat vague. It never occurred to me to research the subject; third-graders do not research, they just draw. So I blundered ahead with my undernourished dragon, and at its completion I was fiercely proud: he was long and green as a cucumber, and somewhat of the same shape. His wide nostrils exhaled blooms of fire. His back was scaly, his serpentine tongue forked. Who could ask for a more splendid dragon?

Yet one morning when I arrived at school (I was always late, even though I lived a block away and most of the others came by school bus from miles out in the country), I possessively glanced to the back of the room to survey my mural and immediately saw it had been ruined. Across the entire length someone (and I knew who) had crudely lettered—in black paint with thick black strokes of the widest brush—the hateful legend:

SAINT GEORGE AND THE ALIGATER

From the horse's rear end dropped what appeared to be great pieces of coal, but which I knew were intended as something else. I became so upset I had to go home. I could think only of the work of months, dozens and dozens of recesses, that had been spent on that mural. Now I could never show it to my parents on Parents' Day in June. Now I could not exhibit it in

the Public Landing Hobby Show, and last year I had taken
first prize in the Juvenile Division for my painting of the
Town Hall, winning a bowl of goldfish that were still my pets.
Now this year's project was ruined. And Righteous hadn't
even spelled alligator correctly. Was it any wonder I hated him
so?

The accident happened just several months later, after summer had fallen in on the town like the roof of a burning barn.
I was sitting at dinner with my parents when the telephone
rang. My mother answered it as always, trying to protect my
father from any unnecessary extractions at night. I paid no
attention to her muffled voice in the next room. I sat greedily
devouring a chicken drumstick that was fried just the way I
liked it, crusty and gleaming with grease (we had never heard
of cholesterol then), and anticipating dessert, which was my
favorite: pineapple upside-down cake with maraschino cherries
on top. When my mother returned to the dining room, I could
see something was wrong. She didn't sit back down at all, but
went to my father's chair and stood behind him, laying a hand
on his shoulder as she did when she had something important
or grave to discuss. My father cocked his head to look at her,
and for a moment she kept the silence. I momentarily stopped
gnawing on the drumstick and waited. "It's the Fellows boy,"
she finally said. "The younger one. Righteous, the one in
Billy's class."

"What about him?" my father asked, sensing the doom in
her voice, looking at me with a frown. I had never told my
parents about my bully problem at school, and I had con-
vinced the teacher not to tell them either. If I was going to be
picked on at school, I didn't want to be picked on at home too.
I figured once my father knew I had a bully problem, he would
keep after me until I had floored the villain before a cheering
crowd. There was no chance of that, so I kept my secret. "What
about the Fellows boy?" my father asked again.

"Drowned," my mother said. Then she put her head in her
hands. When she lifted her head again a few seconds later, she

had a different face. It was as if she had put on a mask, this one white and pinched with pain. "That was Sally Moore on the phone. She heard it from her cleaning woman, who lives out there somewhere near the Fellows' farm. Sally says the boy and his brother went swimming to the millpond today, and the younger one, Righteous, was diving off the spillway. He dove all morning and the last time he just didn't come up at all—" Her voice broke and she buried her head in her hands once more. She reminded me of an ostrich.

"Have they found the body?" my father asked, pushing his full plate away from him and placing his rumpled napkin atop the table.

"They just did. The firemen went down with grappling hooks."

"He must have hit his head on the cement," my father said.

"I don't know. I just don't know."

I resumed eating the drumstick. I didn't say a word, tearing off chunks of dark meat with my good strong teeth. Then I realized my parents were both looking at me.

"Son? Billy? Do you know what we just said? Do you know what a terrible thing has happened?" My father's voice was urgent.

"He doesn't realize, he doesn't realize," my mother murmured.

"Your friend Righteous is dead," my father said, his voice softer now. "You'll never ever see him again. Do you know what that means?"

"Don't call him my friend. He wasn't my friend," I said simply, sitting tall in my chair to avoid a lecture on lordosis. It was marvelous to be able to tell the truth. Suddenly the world was changed.

My mother's mouth had dropped open like a trap door. My father stood up.

"Son! Don't speak disrespectfully of the dead!" he boomed across the bowl of mashed potatoes.

"I'm glad he's dead, I'm glad, I'm glad!" I chanted, relief

flooding my body. "He wasn't my friend, he was nasty and I'm glad he's gone." Flitting through my mind were entire afternoons of what school would be like next autumn, without Righteous: no Righteous lurking on the playground, no Righteous to jam me into the supply closet. . . . Suddenly I could be myself. Suddenly school would be fun again. "I'm glad he's dead," I repeated, equating dead with gone and gone with good riddance.

"I hope, I trust, we hear you incorrectly?" my father shouted.

"It's the shock," my mother said. "He doesn't know what he's saying. They used to play together—"

"We'll hope not. We'll just hope he doesn't know what he's saying," my father said, glaring at me. "You go to your room immediately, young man, and think about what you've been saying."

"But, sir," I protested, suddenly realizing the consequences of my outburst. "What about dessert? My pineapple upside-down cake? Mother made it especially for me!"

"Good God! There's a boy dead in this town tonight, and all you can think about is your dessert. God help us, son. Get out of my sight. This instant. You make me sick!"

It was no use, I knew, so I slowly got up from the table and left the room. On my way out I looked beseechingly at my mother. Maybe she would intervene, or at least bring some of the cake to my room. But the minute my eyes caught hers, she turned her head. She avoided my look entirely, so I ran for the flight of carpeted stairs.

Once in my room, I did exactly what I wanted to do. My father had told me to think about what I had said, but there was nothing to think about. Instead, I lay on the bed and listened to the radio. I lay there for a long time, listening to program after program—"Can You Top This?," "Peter Salem," "Sam Spade," "Nick Carter," "The Shadow." After "The Shadow" some junk came on, so I turned off the radio. The silence of the house was deafening. What room were they in, my parents? I had not been aware of my mother's light rustling or my father's heavy voice for what seemed hours. I was aware only of my acute disappointment at being deprived of the cake. I plotted ways to sneak downstairs in the middle of the night, when I was certain my parents were abed, to snitch a slice. Already I suffered imaginary hunger pangs. Finally, restless, I turned my attention to my prize bowl of goldfish flickering brightly on my dresser.

There were five of them, four large orange ones and one small gray, which I thought of as the baby goldfish, though it was probably a full-grown fish of an altogether different variety. I had already fed the fish earlier that day, but to amuse myself I fed them again. Somebody in the family might as well not go hungry, I thought with self-pity. The fish swam to the top and began eating with amusing kissing motions. The goldfish never failed to interest me, their fins waving like disheveled rags, their gills opening and closing like fireplace grates, their reflectionless eyes round in surprise. After the food was gone, I lay back on the bed and for the first time since dinner I thought of Righteous. Immediately in my mind's eye I saw his leering face and his blackened tooth. Then I shut him out entirely. As I fell asleep, I concluded we were all better off now that he was dead.

I slept until it was deeply morning. Only when my mother tapped on the door and brought in a breakfast tray did I open my eyes. The sun was quite high in the sky.

"You needed a good rest, so we let you sleep," she said, putting the tray across my lap in the bed. "You had quite a shock last night. You worried your father and me." Before I looked at the tray, I knew what it held: orange juice, a glass of milk, and the biggest slice of pineapple upside-down cake I had ever seen. "I guess it won't hurt you for breakfast," she sighed, seeing me prong the cake quickly with my fork. "I know how you love it so."

I didn't say anything, merely eating the cake as quickly as possible. I felt as if I hadn't eaten in a week.

"Your father and I hope you've thought about everything you said last night, and that you are sorry," she said, smoothing down my hair where it stuck off in a rooster's tail in back.

"Yes," I said between mouthfuls. "I'm sorry."

"That's better. It was a terrible thing that happened."

"Yes," I said again, thinking it was nothing terrible at all. Then, out of the corner of my eye, I saw them, the goldfish. My head swiveled toward the bowl, and I could scarcely believe what I saw. All five fish floated on their sides on top of the water. They could have been wood chips on a pond, lying perfectly flat, perfectly still.

"My fish!" I cried. My mother looked then, too. She crossed the room quickly and silently, gliding as if on casters. She took one look into the bowl and then looked back at me.

"What did you do to them, Billy?" she asked.

"Do? I didn't do anything. They were fine last night, swimming and bobbing and eating—"

"You fed them last night?"

"Sure. They were hungry. You should have seen them go at it!"

"But you had fed them in the afternoon. I saw you do it."

"That doesn't matter. They were still hungry."

"It does matter. It matters very much. Don't you see what you did? You overfed and killed them. The fish are *dead*." Her voice was full of sorrow.

Dead? Was that what caused the beautiful flickering to stop? Was that what caused the fish to lie on their sides like so many chips of wood? I slipped off the bed and stared into the bowl. Already the bright scales seemed to have tarnished. Their grand mandarin beards and tails were still. It was then that I thought of Righteous Fellows. It was then that I saw him, lying on his pale side somewhere in the millpond, Righteous also perfectly still, never again to move or talk or breathe, never to dive into the sun-filled pond. It was then that I got sick on my pineapple upside-down cake, and I have never been able to touch a slice of it since.

In a Country
of Strangers

The day her *True Romance* didn't come in the mail Dola suspicioned something. Things began to fall into place then, seemingly isolated incidents like a missing insurance coupon, a strange noise in the night. Now the magazine: *True Romance* always arrived the last Friday of the month, and this Friday when she returned to the apartment house, expecting to find it in her mailbox—eagerly anticipating it, in fact, planning to read it while soaking her tired feet in a bucket of hot Epsom salts—the box was empty. She stood in the foyer for a long time, staring through the little glass window of the empty box, and finally she opened it with her key and poked a hand around inside, just to make sure. Then, drowning in disappointment, she went to the building superintendent's apartment.

"You do anything with my *True Romance?*" she asked Mr. O'Shay. The superintendent stood in the doorway. Over his shoulder she could see a half-empty bottle of booze on the floor by the sagging sofa, and she clucked disapproval. Not outwardly, only inwardly: she was never one to criticize others, no matter how much they deserved it.

"Did I do anything with your *what?*" he asked, scratching his knobby chest and peering at her through watery eyes. He looked just like a monkey she had seen once in the Bronx Zoo.

"My *True Romance!* It's a magazine, full of stories. It was supposed to be in my mail today!" she shouted. Then, seeing Mrs. O'Shay cringing in the crowded little kitchen beyond, Dola lowered her voice. Every time she knocked on the O'Shays' door—which wasn't often, she didn't like to be beholden, even if it was his job to fix the heat or wiring or whatever whenever it went bad—she could smell cabbage cooking. Mrs. O'Shay seemed always to be cooking cabbage. Smelling it then, on the day she lost her *True Romance,* Dola suddenly experienced grief rather than outrage. Grief for the sorrows that were poverty. Cabbage was subsistence for poor white trash. Back home in Public Landing, even she and her papa and Hyacinth had eaten better than that, even between canning seasons when the factory was shut down and they were all out of work!

So she didn't question Mr. O'Shay further. He led a sad life. She said the magazine most likely had been delayed, or lost in the mail, and she went upstairs to her apartment where she broiled a nice pork chop and tossed a good garden salad full of avocado, black olives, and garlic. She would do without some things, but she would never deprive her gizzard. *You are what you eat,* she once had read, and she knew it was so. She felt better when she ate better. The food consoled her on the loss of her favorite magazine.

Her suspicions were confirmed the following week when *Jet* and *Ebony* failed to arrive. When she had no mail all week except for bills, she knew she had been right. After all, her subscriptions were paid in full; her mailbox was under lock and key. Somehow, someone was stealing from her. She felt she ought to see Mr. O'Shay, though talking to that man was like arguing with a pair of mismatched Missouri mules.

She went to his apartment and was about to knock when she hesitated before the door. She was positive she smelled bacon frying. The O'Shays were having bacon, as expensive as that was these days! Then it occurred to her that whoever was stealing her mail had hired Mr. O'Shay to do it. After all, he had keys to all the apartments and mailboxes in the building. Of course. That was how the O'Shays could now eat bacon instead of cabbage. She could never trust him again. She resolved to rent a box in the post office the very next day, so at least her mail would be safe.

Except the post office man said No. He looked her square in the eye and said there wasn't a box available. Said they were all rented. Dola stared at the long, long wall of metal boxes, row upon row of boxes, and knew he was lying. He must be in on it too. He must be one of the ones playing tricks on her. She hadn't expected their influence to extend to the post office. Maybe it was someone in the post office all along, and not Mr. O'Shay. She couldn't be sure of anything.

"You must have one empty box," she said, feeling futility seep thick as molasses into her bones.

"I'm sorry, but we don't," the man said.

"You can't tell me that! I've got rights! You think I don't got rights?"

"It's not a matter of rights, Madam. There simply isn't an unrented box to be had. Now, if you'd like to leave your name and address, we'll be happy to contact you when one is available . . ." His skin was white and bland as a pudding, and his hair was shot through with dandruff. Dandruff had cascaded upon the shoulders of his blue suit and he didn't have sense enough to brush it away. He just let it lie there for all the world to see, which told Dola right away he hadn't a grain of self-respect.

"Don't tell me that! It's a lie and you know it's a lie. Us poor people has rights too."

"Why don't you fill out this form, and we'll be glad to see what we . . ."

She pushed away the pen he extended. "Not gonna fill out no forms. My name's on too many forms already! Social Security forms. Insurance forms. Unemployment forms. Credit Bureau forms. Forms, forms, forms! All you want is for me to sign so you can use it against me. Get more money out of me somehow. Most likely you'll study my handwriting and forge checks in my name too. That's probably why my bank account is all messed up right now!" Her feet were planted wide apart and her heavy wicker handbag hung upon her arm. She leaned far forward and looked intently into the man's blue eyes, reducing the space between them, the gulf that separated them, all the while feeling perspiration accumulating beneath her platinum-blond wig. "I know who you are and who you're with. You're one of *them,* all right," she said softly, right into his face. He had foul breath. You'd think he could afford a fifteen-cent package of Sen-Sen. She turned and wobbled on her high heels toward the tall glass door that would let her escape into the churning streets.

She had wanted to slide the handbag down her arm, to hold it by the handle and swing it around and around over her head like she had seen Steve Reeves do with a chain on the television. She would swing the handbag around and then let the post-office man have it smack in the face. She would clobber him with it and it would serve him right, the two-faced Judas. Bobby Kennedy had an office right in this very post-office building, yet this man refused to rent her a box. She should have gone upstairs and complained to Bobby Kennedy. She should tell Bobby Kennedy people were pestering her. Or hit that man with her bag. But she did neither. She was a peaceful woman, a good Christian, and Jesus said *Do unto others as you would have others do unto you,* and Dr. King had said *No violence, no violence.* So the heavy handbag remained on her arm and she made her way out the door, fighting back the terrible outrage that threatened to overwhelm her in the dazzling August light.

Teetering on her heels, Dola slowly made her way down the great stone steps of the post-office building. Perspiration rivered down her sides from her talcumed armpits, and beneath the savage sun her mind reeled like buzzards circling overhead. How long had it been since she had last seen buzzards on the horizon? Over twenty years. When she left Public Landing with her cardboard Woolworth suitcase, to come to this Sodom and Gomorrah city. Ugly as they were, the buzzards, their raw necks tilted forward like Grandfather's on a front porch, she would welcome the sight of one now. She would embrace a buzzard and call it Brother. Because the man had said *No.* Because he was one of them. Someone had even enlisted the post office of these United States of America against her, had bribed the man with money or a fifth of cheap whisky.

Before bed that night, she got down on her knees and prayed to sweet Jesus for help and understanding. She prayed that she would come to know why someone should be tormenting her. It flickered through her mind that it might be because she had sent a contribution to the S.N.C.C. Then she lay there wondering if that could be so. She considered writing Stokely Carmichael and telling him her contribution was a mistake, that she wanted her money back. But she would be ashamed to do that. And it probably was too late anyhow, the check had been cashed, the money collected. As she fell asleep she decided she must be exaggerating everything.

The next day was Mrs. Cohn's day. Mrs. Cohn never washed a dish from one week to the next, so that Dola had to wash and dry a week's worth of dishes in addition to cleaning the entire apartment and doing whatever ironing Mrs. Cohn had left for her. The other people Dola worked for, the other days of the week, at least they weren't that lazy. At least they did most of their own dishes. But not Mrs. Cohn. She lived on Park Avenue, had a fancy big apartment and a fancy little dog, but she let her dishes pile up all over the countertops. Whenever Dola let herself into the apartment, she would smell them, those heaps of sour dishes with dried egg yolks and sticky beets and congealed gravy. Just smelling them was enough to gag a vulture, but Mrs. Cohn waltzed around in her diamonds as if her kitchen smelled like Chanel Number Five.

Today when Dola let herself in, she saw the Cohns had given a party the night before. The kitchen counters and sink were full of dirty glasses—martini glasses and whisky-sour glasses and highball glasses—many with thick lipstick prints or disintegrated cigarette butts floating inside. It took her a good two hours longer to get everything done, but finally the apartment was clean, the glasses dried and put away. Just before she left, she knocked on Mrs. Cohn's bedroom door. The woman always lay in bed all afternoon when Dola was there, sipping Scotch and reading *Harper's Bazaar* and the *New Yorker*.

"Yes, Dola? What is it?" Mrs. Cohn's eyes examined her through little glasses shaped just like the ones Benjamin Franklin wore in a picture book Dola had seen once. Now, why would any woman today want glasses like Benjamin Franklin wore? There was just no accounting.

"Miz Cohn, I just want to ask you somethin'. You're one understanding white woman, and you know what makes things happen in this world—"

"Things? What things, Dola dear? Do speak up. Don't mumble so."

"Yes ma'am. What I want to know is, about a contribution? I didn't mean any harm by it. I just thought . . . I just thought I was in a position to help. Do you think any white folks would take offense at Dola sending off a little money . . ."

"Contribution? White folks?" Mrs. Cohn's eyes drifted back to the open magazine in her lap. "Oh, yes, the contribution. Is it really time for your church's fund-raising drive again? Time flies, Dola, time does fly. I'll give you Mr. Cohn's contribution next week, okay? He likes to enter it on his books, because it's tax deductible, you know. . . . Did you remember to clean out the toilet bowl this time?"

"Yes ma'am."

"I'll bet. Your check is on the hall table. Do double-lock the door after you, won't you, dear?"

The elevator door slid soundlessly open and Dola stepped out into the red and gold lobby downstairs. She stopped before the baroque mirror on the wall and patted her platinum wig to make sure it was firmly in place. The wig gleamed in the artificial light. Dola smiled. That was some wig, that was. It had taken over a week's earnings, but it was worth it. She gave one of the soft blond curls a loving pat before turning away from the reflection. On her way out, she greeted the uniformed doorman.

The sidewalk was almost deserted. Nearly everyone else was home for dinner. Dola realized how hungry she was. Mrs. Cohn's refrigerator was usually so empty, Dola was ashamed to make herself lunch. She just ate a few crackers and drank some skimmed milk instead. But today there hadn't even been any milk. The only bottles in the refrigerator were quinine water and collins mix, left over from the party. Dola wouldn't touch those. Cocktails were temptations of the Devil.

She stood for a moment before the apartment house and contemplated hailing a cab. She always took the subway home, but today she was so tired she didn't think she could face the heat and the noise. The work and the worry had been too much today. To sit back just once and have a shiny cab whisk her uptown like a limousine—that would be the life! Then she frowned. Cab fare would eat up nearly half the day's wages; she couldn't afford that kind of foolishness. Something must be ailing her to even consider it. She started walking toward the

subway entrance. Then it happened. She leaped back, terrified, and stood shaking. Everything had gone out of focus, and
she kept staring at the big object that now lay mangled before
her on the pavement.

"Good God! Are you all right?" It was the doorman, his
hands on her shoulders, shaking her roughly.

She raised her eyes and saw that he was flour white. It had
terrified him too, even though he was yards away and behind
the thick glass door. It hadn't fallen directly before him.

"I'm all right, I reckon," she said. Her tongue was thick and
felt swollen in her head, like it did when the dentist stuck a
needle in her gum.

"You could have been killed!" he cried, still holding onto
her.

"I know that. Don't you think I know that?" she cried. She
pulled away from his sturdy grasp.

Together they stood looking down at the air-conditioning
unit on the sidewalk, huge and gray and out of place, like
some whale washed ashore and dead on the beach. The metal
case was now all buckled and crazily bent. Its metal fiber filter
spilled out like guts.

"I don't see how it could happen," the doorman said. "All
those bolts and screws and things. They'd all have to be loose
for it to fall—"

A small crowd gathered. One man even came out of the
apartment house in his silk bathrobe and slippers. "What's all
the commotion, huh?" he barked, his mustache bobbing up
and down. Nobody answered him. Then he saw the air conditioner and said, "What's that thing doing there?" He craned
his neck to stare up the side of the building, and then they all
did, their heads turned upward and mouths open like baby
birds in a nest, everyone trying to determine which window
was minus its air conditioner. Everyone looked up except Dola.
She knew where it came from. It came from Mrs. Cohn's apartment! She was one of them too! She knew all along what con-

tribution Dola was talking about! Dola closed her eyes and said
softly, "They tried to kill me." Her body trembled like a dry
autumn leaf.

The heads jerked downward now and the crowd stared at
her. They were white people, every one of them. "Somebody
just tried to *kill* me," she repeated.

"Come now, it was just an accident. These things happen
every day in New York," the doorman said, looking nervous
and wiping his brow as if afraid he would somehow lose his job
as a result of the occurrence. "It must be the vibrations from
traffic loosened the bolts somehow. . . ."

"Do you want the police? Shall I call the police?" the man in
the bathrobe asked importantly.

"Don't want no police," Dola said positively. Then she
raised her voice. "Call me a cab. I just want to get myself
home. I got to get away from here!"

Once inside the cab, she fell into a trance. Even the expensive tick-tick of the meter did not disturb her brooding. Only
once did she stop meditating on what had just happened, and
that was to take out her compact and look into its mirror. Her
insides were crawling and she wanted to see if she looked any
different on the outside. But the eyes that stared back at her
were serene: big brown calm eyes, the pupils flecked with gold.
That was what people on the street saw, that was what Mrs.
Cohn saw: a big, calm colored lady. Well dressed, even a wig
upon her head. Happy as a clam. No one else in the world
knew that something was eating her insides away, that something had started as cold suspicion like ice in her bowels, then
turned to apprehension, and now was fear. Someone was actually after her life. They weren't just giving her a rough time
now; they had nearly murdered her on Park Avenue in broad
daylight! Mr. O'Shay, Mrs. Cohn, the post-office man, they
were all in on it. She studied herself in the little oval mirror,
but the reflected face still looked the same. It exchanged with

her the same long, confident gaze. She snapped the compact
closed and returned to her ruminations.

When the taxi stopped opposite her building, she paid the
driver and quickly scurried across the pavement. She carried
her handbag in her fist as a weapon, but no one approached
her. Inside the lobby all the faces looked familiar, but she took
no chances, she hurried past them all, past the mailboxes that
she had come to despise, and took the self-service elevator to
her floor.

She was out of breath when she let herself in, and she kicked
her shoes off. Then she raced to the living-room window and
raised her arm to lower the shade. Hesitating for a moment,
before shutting out the cruel sunlight, she turned and surveyed
the room. Here she was safe. It was hers, all hers. She had
picked it out and paid for it on time, arranged it all herself.
She could never have had it if she had let herself get hooked
years before, to have children and a shiftless husband lying
around all day. She studied them, the long white sofa with its
blond wood legs; the kidney-shaped coffee table that looked so
modern; the matching pair of white chairs on the fluffy sky-
blue rug. It was all hers. She had worked for years to be able to
move into this kind of building in this kind of neighborhood,
mostly a white neighborhood, away from all the uptown riff-
raff. (Was *that* why they were after her? she wondered frantically.) She had never invited another soul into the apartment.
Because then it wouldn't be exclusively hers. And other people
would ruin it. They would drop cigarette ashes on the beautiful rug. Burn holes in the sofa upholstery. Leave wet rings
from their glasses on the blond coffee table. The only person
who had even seen the apartment was Mr. O'Shay, who had
once come to fix the radiator. Dola had been proud for him to
see it, to see how high on the hog she really lived. She lived
much better than the O'Shays, and they were white Irish Cath-
olics who had always lived in the North. They had had advan-
tages she hadn't.

She latched the window on the inside before drawing the shade. Then she padded in her stockinged feet into the bedroom and latched that window too, and pulled the shade down even with the sill. She carefully removed her wig and placed it on its stand on the dresser top. She stroked its silky soft tresses and tried not to look at her own coarse, close-cropped hair in the dresser mirror. She kept it cut so short she looked like a day-old pickaninny. Suddenly she realized she had not even locked the front door! She ran through the hallway, nearly slipping on the heavily waxed hardwood floor, and reached the door short of wind. She bolted it with one strong flick of the wrist.

Then she began the nightly ritual of preparing dinner. Tonight it didn't take long. There was cole slaw left from the night before, some cold ham, and a few pickles floating in the bottom of their glass jar in the back of the refrigerator. It wasn't much of a meal but it was all she wanted. The narrow escape from death had taken her appetite. She felt as if a hand in a red rubber glove had gripped her guts. She closed her eyes and thought, *My skull could have been split wide open. My brains would have spilled out like peas from a pod. They would make little popping sounds as they hit the sidewalk. I would be lying on Park Avenue right now, and somebody would have found my wallet in my bag, found the card with Hyacinth's name and phone number on it. That was why I insisted Hyacinth have a phone all these years, why I paid the phone bill for her every month. So that whenever they call her, they can reach her. So she can start the funeral plans.*

One of the first things Dola had done after settling in the city and finding a job was to take out a five-thousand-dollar life-insurance policy. So if anything happened to her, her sister Hyacinth wouldn't have to pay to bury her. It would be expensive business: shipping her body back to Public Landing by train, the funeral, the flowers, the coffin, the lace negligee to be laid out in. It would all cost a good three thousand dollars to do it right, she reckoned, even if Miss Mahalia Jackson didn't charge anything to sing. (That was one of the special clauses in the will, that Hyacinth write the singer immediately and ask Mahalia Jackson to sing "The Lord's Prayer" over Dola's grave.) Any money left over would give her sister something to remember her by. Hyacinth's husband had gone off and left her years ago and now she was alone with their papa, a bent-over old man who wouldn't eat a mouthful except oatmeal with blackstrap molasses poured over it. Hyacinth had no money, nothing except her pride. And Dola had always paid her own way in this world, she always would. Since it was her own pigheaded notion to get herself up north, to leave the bosom of the family and live among strangers, she couldn't expect her sister to pay crating expenses to get her back to be buried where she belonged, where she should have stayed to begin with.

Carrying the ham on its platter to the table, Dola suddenly staggered against one of the dinette chairs and barked her shin on the cold chrome leg. *Got to get myself to bed,* she moaned softly in the silent room, rubbing her shinbone as she sat down. Her body sagged in the chair like a sack of wheat. *This girl got to get to bed. And tomorrow she's got to figure out what to do. Before it's too late. Maybe she should leave this neighborhood, this city even, and go back to Public Landing. Buy another wig, another color, and travel in disguise.*

From the first mouthful, she knew the cole slaw was funny. It hadn't spoiled, she'd bought it fresh at the delicatessen the day before. But it tasted bitter, more bitter than cabbage salad should taste. She took another forkful, just to be sure, and while she munched on its shredded bitterness it occurred to her what it was: They had put LSD in her food! They had. They were putting dope in her food, perhaps had been putting it there for some time. That explained why she felt so tired, why she fell against chairs and felt so hemmed in on the subway! They were poisoning her system, slowly but surely. They weren't even content to poison just her body—they were poisoning her mind as well! That cole slaw was chock full of LSD.

Just the day before she had seen in the *Daily News* where some dope fiend had given a young girl a dose of LSD and she had gone plumb out of her little mind. *My God, my God, LSD in the cole slaw!* Dola screamed to the four walls. *Poison!*

She unbolted the door and ran into the hall. She would find the police. That was it. There was usually a policeman down the street somewhere, she would find him. He would help. But when she reached the elevator, a strange man stood there, a hulking man she had never seen on her floor or even in the building before. He wore a blue suit and just before she wheeled around to run back into her apartment she thought she could see an avalanche of dandruff on his shoulders.

Her door was wide open, just as she had left it. It didn't matter. They could get in now anyhow, whether she locked it or not. They had gotten in to poison her food with drugs, they could do anything. One of them was out there by the elevator right now, waiting for her.

She ran to the window and clawed at the shade. It wouldn't raise properly and finally she grabbed hold frantically and ripped it in two. The top half shuddered and dangled from its roller like a lynched man. Someone was loitering on the corner beneath her window, by the lamppost, smoking a cigarette and looking at his watch. It was a man in a dark suit, and just as she saw him he stared up at her window, directly at her window and into her face as she leaned forward. His eyes met hers and they said, *We know you're there. We know you're there and we're out to get you. For good this time. You've overstepped the line—*

Dola heard a strange gurgling in her throat, an animal sound, and she felt the cords writhe in her neck like snakes. But that was all of a scream she could manage now. Late daylight poured into the apartment, exposing in its slant the white sofa and the powder-blue rug, exposing Dola at the window, arms dangling uselessly at her sides like a broken marionette's, and she realized it was impossible to hide any longer— she had torn the shade.

A
Boy's
Tale

The morning after Mr. Winter died, the boy Randal said to his mother, "I've gotta go read the funny papers to Mrs. Winter." And his mother didn't understand at all. But Randal did. He knew he had to do it.

The Winters and their cats lived in a dark-brown shingled house on Cedar Street. Outwardly it was like many of the other dark, nondescript houses set in a row on that street, only seeming more dark and dismal than the others because the Winters were old and economical and rarely used more than one lamp at a time. Their one extravagance was to leave a night light on in the downstairs hall every evening. Mr. Winter once asked Mrs. Winter who the night light was for, since they never turned it on until they were ready for bed, and turned it off in the morning when the sun was up. Was it for the burglars to see better? he had asked. But Mrs. Winter continued to have her night light, just as she kept her Grandfather Thomas's elegant but wicked-looking sword and saber crossed above the inside of the front door, despite the fact that her visitors always scurried in hunchback through the doorway, scared one of the swords would fall and pinion them upon the floor boards.

Randal lived next door to the Winters, and he knew about Mr. Winter's objections to the night light just as he knew many things about the cantankerous old man. Mrs. Winter confided these little secrets on many of his visits, and that was one of the things that made his talks with Mrs. Winter so enjoyable: the feeling of sharing some clandestine knowledge about the dark old bushy-browed man he disliked. His parents never shared any secrets with him. Mrs. Winter did not mean to make fun of her husband before the boy—surely she merely enjoyed company; it relieved the boredom of old age, and she was happy to rattle on and on about how Ira spilled this and Ira had a fit about that. Randal relished it all. Once he pointed out that Mr. Winter had mashed potatoes stuck all over the bottom of his tie. Mrs. Winter inspected the tie and then she and the boy laughed and laughed, while Mr. Winter merely sat in the stout armchair and silently twisted his bony ankle around and around in half circles.

But Mr. Winter had not always been silent, especially on the subject of cats. Randal thought Mrs. Winter had had more cats during her lifetime than he would ever *see* in his. She always had five or six at one time, and when one would leave or die, she somehow would manage to find another to replace it. People knew if they left their unwanted cat in front of Mrs. Winter's house, it would have a good home. Randal thought it must be nice, having all those cats—his mother would never let him have a pet. But Mr. Winter was always cursing them. If he came downstairs and found one in his favorite chair, he would yell and strike out at it with his knobby cane. Randal had never seen Mr. Winter actually hit one of the cats—he somehow always missed. But Mrs. Winter told of the time Mr. Winter had broken a tomcat's back with one swing of his cane. The boy could always conjure up a pitiful image of the broke-back cat whenever he wanted to feel particularly uncharitable toward Mr. Winter.

But then, the Winters' house did have a peculiar odor, which his mother attributed to the cats. Every room downstairs smelled the same way. He never mentioned the smell to Mrs. Winter, and she never mentioned it to him, so he supposed she didn't mind it. Sometimes she burned incense in the corner, on top of the big old radio with the crackled, horny-yellow dial. Then for a while the whole downstairs smelled like wet boxwood, an odor Randal knew and loved. He thought boxwood, after a rain, had a clear, clean odor. Once he hid inside a big boxwood shrub during a game of hide-and-seek. The shrubbery had been wet, but he didn't mind, even when water trickled coldly down his neck, it all smelled so fresh. Perhaps that was why Mr. Winter used to sit back in the dark corner all the time, to be close to the incense. He probably made Mrs. Winter buy it to get rid of the cat odor.

All the times the boy came visiting the Winters' house, he and Mr. Winter had never been able to talk. He was a huge ruddy man who picked at his ear with the end of a wooden matchstick. He would jam the stick into his ear and then make horrible faces, as if in great pain because of what he had done. The boy never liked to watch Mr. Winter's fierce expressions. He was a tough old man. Mrs. Winter said he had survived terrible sieges of both chickahominy and quinsy. Once his tongue was so swollen in his head the doctor said he'd have to cut it out. Mr. Winter had mumbled, "Be damned!" and he soon got well. But sometimes Randal wondered what need Mr. Winter had of a tongue, he talked so seldom.

Mr. Winter had been a lighthouse keeper at Cape Henlopen. At first that fact excited the boy's imagination. What fun to have your own lighthouse all to yourself! Randal imagined himself walking circuitously about the high deck, his chest out, his face whipped by the wind as he scanned the horizon for ships. It was a known fact that old Mrs. Winter wasn't afraid of any of the hurricanes and electrical storms that rage on the peninsula at each summer's end. She had seen too many storms and high tides in her day to be frightened.

Hanging directly above Mr. Winter's chair was a fly-specked lithograph of the Henlopen lighthouse in a black frame. Mrs. Winter said the picture had been made from a sketch her aunt had done while at a picnic. On the balcony near the top of the lighthouse was a black spot that Mrs. Winter always insisted was her husband looking out to sea. There was no sign of Mrs. Winter in the picture. Randal would not believe it really was Mr. Winter, and, if it were, he was willing to bet the old man was standing there picking at his ear and making faces. Whenever Randal visited the Winters now he never looked at the picture. It wasn't fair for someone like Mr. Winter to have had all that fun. Why couldn't he and Mrs. Winter have been there together, instead? The cellar of the lighthouse would have been full of her canned foods and preserves and lots of candy for the winter. Finally he rationalized that it wouldn't be so wonderful, stuck out there in the middle of the ocean with no movies to see.

So he never talked much to Mr. Winter. Probably the old man's years at sea had taught him how really little speech is necessary to survive in this world. Randal's visits were filled largely with telling Mrs. Winter about his grades in school, what films were playing at the Saturday matinee at the Bijou, or about a library book he was reading. Sometimes they talked politics, too, though once he had confused Mr. Stassen with Mr. Stalin, since he had seen both names in the newspapers about the same time. Every Sunday morning Mrs. Winter read the funny papers to him. They both knew he could read them better than she. She read very slowly, working at it, and every now and then would pronounce words incorrectly. But there was something nice about hearing her read aloud, and he hoped she would do it forever.

Mrs. Winter often apologized for her reading. "I am an

only child," she once said, bemusing Randal with this refer-
ence to herself as a child, "and I was taught at home by my
mother and my grandfather. All my education was in the home
until I was eleven. I think that's why I've always been such a
poor reader and bad at figures. Mother taught me religion, and
Grandfather taught me nautical terms and how to jig."

Mrs. Winter never forgot to give him his surprise from the
bowl in the dining room. Not even once. Whenever he got
ready to leave, she would kiss him on the forehead and pinch
his cheek, and then say, "Now, let me see. . . ." Then she
would toddle off to the dining room. She always kept her surprises in the white milk-glass bowl centered on the dining-
room table. Sometimes it was candy, but most of the time it
was fresh fruit. Randal had a sweet tooth, and he used to hope
it was candy, but fruit was sweet too, and didn't melt all over
his fingers in the summertime like the chocolate bars she gave
him. No matter how gingerly he handled them, the chocolate
always went soft in his hands before he was through eating.
One time Mrs. Winter must have forgotten to go to the store,
because she came back with a tomato instead of fruit or candy.
He had taken that home to his mother, disappointed, until she
told him the important thing was that Mrs. Winter had
wanted to give him something even when there was so little in
the house.

Each time he thanked Mrs. Winter for the surprise, and
each time she said he was welcome she was sure. And in the last
months, when Mr. Winter was so sick and stayed upstairs in
his cast-iron bed, Randal, just before he left, would ask how Mr.
Winter was. Mrs. Winter would always say, "Not too good,"
and her eyes would shift to the lighthouse picture above the
empty easy chair. The boy would avert his eyes to keep from
having to look at the beautiful tower, the image of Mr. Winter's own private lighthouse. Randal supposed she didn't have
any other picture of Mr. Winter at all—if that spot really was
Mr. Winter at the railing, which the boy doubted with all his
heart.

Then the morning after Mr. Winter died, Randal said to his mother, "I've gotta go read the funny papers to Mrs. Winter."

"What?" his mother had asked. There was a time when no matter what he would tell his mother, she would always ask back, "What?" as if he spoke an entirely foreign language.

"I said I've gotta go read the funny papers to Mrs. Winter."

But his mother didn't understand. She had to understand, because he knew that it was something he just *had* to do.

"You know Mrs. Winter always reads the funny papers to me every Sunday morning," he reminded her. "Every Sunday morning she reads to me, right after Sunday school. You know that."

"Yes, dear, I know. But this morning is different. Poor old Mr. Winter died in his sleep last night. Mrs. Winter can't read to you today."

"But I didn't say I wanted *her* to read to *me*," he told his mother. *"I'm* going to read to *her*. The funny papers. To make her laugh. Don't you see?"

"It's the same thing," his mother said. "There are some things you just don't understand yet. One of them is that you do not try to make people laugh when someone they love has just died."

Randal could not see that at all. He thought that that would be the very time people would want to be made to laugh, to get their minds away from things like people dying and deep holes in the ground (which was where they put dead people, he knew). When his mother told him to go upstairs to get out of his Sunday suit and change into play clothes, he didn't do it. He grabbed the thick *Sunday Inquirer* with all the funny papers and went next door to Mrs. Winter's house.

It was a clear winter day, not a day for dying, a day bright with snow and tangerines and starlings. He carried the paper under his arm and knocked on the door with a wool-mittened fist. Some strange woman let him in without saying a word. The woman pointed to Mrs. Winter sitting in the living room, and then she left the boy and rejoined some other strangers sitting around the kitchen table covered with crackled oil cloth. They were all drinking coffee and talking in low voices.

Mrs. Winter didn't look much different to Randal. She wasn't crying loudly or pulling her hair or shredding things as he had seen widows do in the movies. He didn't know exactly what he had expected her to look like that morning, but he had expected to find some metamorphosis. Now, seeing her, he was sure it was all right to read to her as he had planned.

Before she had a chance to tell him that she didn't feel like reading to him, he turned on the floor lamp and sat down next to her. Mrs. Winter looked at him with wondering eyes and she blinked as they became accustomed to the light in the dim room. Randal started reading in a deliberate manner, and one of the men from the kitchen quickly came to the door and looked in to see what was going on. But the boy didn't pay any attention. He continued reading, going through "Maggie and Jiggs" and "Gasoline Alley" and "The Little King" and all the ones he knew she always laughed at the most. After a time the stranger from the kitchen went back to the coffee drinkers and then everything was fine.

At first Mrs. Winter just sat there, with a cat in her lap, and her big gray head drooped down on her chest as if she weren't enjoying the reading. She stared at her sturdy black oxford shoes. Whenever he passed the paper to her so she could see the funny pictures, she would look and nod her sad gray head and not say anything. But by the time he had read "Little Iodine," she was chuckling almost as she always did, and she said, "That Little Iodine is really something, really a sight, she is." And Randal said, yes, she really was a sight, and that Mrs. Winter ought to see what-all Donald Duck was up to that day!

After he gathered the papers that were spread about the floor and squirmed into his mackinaw to leave, Mrs. Winter kissed him on the forehead and said, "Now, let me see . . ." and went into the dining room. That day, the day after Mr.

Winter died, she came back with an apple. The relatives in the kitchen watched her come and go, but they didn't say a word. Then Randal thanked her, and she thanked him, and he started to leave.

He had just reached the front door when he turned and deliberately asked, "How is Mr. Winter today?" The thought of asking had plagued him since he had entered the house clutching the newspapers to cheer the old woman who was finally alone. He had stared at the lighthouse in the picture and the vengeful idea jabbed his brain, like the feel of a vaccination needle, quick and pricking. He knew he should feel sad, but somehow he was glad now to have Mrs. Winter all to himself. Then, after he had asked it, standing in the doorway beneath Captain Thomas's saber and sword, he wished the sword would fall directly and chop off his head. God should let loose the sword. He put his hand to his mouth and looked into Mrs. Winter's eyes. She didn't say anything for a moment, peering at him curiously through her steel-rimmed glasses, and then she said, "Why, he's fine now. Now he's just fine." She smiled weakly with her thin mouth, but there was no smile in her eyes. She had the look Randal had felt on his own face when he was caught doing something he knew he shouldn't do. She looked guilty.

Randal hurried out the door. He left, tugging on his mittens and trying to keep hold of the polished red apple and the rumpled Sunday papers at the same time. He ran through snow the short distance to his house, up to his room, and all the time he thought about her eyes when he had asked about Mr. Winter. He put the apple in his dresser drawer and kept it there for days. He kept it until the skin had gotten wrinkled and brown and the bottom was soft and mushy. His mother found it when she was putting clean socks in the drawer and she made him throw it out. He wanted to cry when she found it, and he never had a more difficult time parting with anything than he did with that little shriveled-up apple. It had made a small wet spot in the bottom of the drawer where it had lain, and after the apple was gone he would go to the drawer and look at the dark, moist place on the wood until that, too, dried up and he couldn't even see it.

Then Randal closed the drawer and lay on his bed. He tried to cry but couldn't. He had always been able to cry before, any time he felt like it. Now he wanted to cry because he couldn't bring himself to go next door again. There would be no more sessions with the funny papers, no more surprises from the milk-glass bowl. Whenever he saw Mrs. Winter bent over her broom, sweeping away the snow from her front steps or bringing in bottles of milk or letting out the cats, he would not stop to chat. He would rush into his house, ashamed, away from her eyes. That portion of his life which was Mrs. Winter had been thrown away, like the bruised and browning apple that, until its final decay and disappearance, had replaced the bright original.

The
Dictates of
the Heart

(For Mr. Roscoe and in memory of Miss Katie)

"Now, I don't mean to force you to a hasty decision," Elmer said to Fannie, fidgeting his big red hands together. "But since Mom's passed on I reckon it's time I commenced to thinking about marriage." He cleared his throat. "And I'd be powerful pleased and honored if you'd consent to be my wife."

His painful speech over, Elmer got off his knees, abandoning that absurd posture, and resumed his place beside her on the sofa. Fannie stared down at her high-buttoned shoes and felt the burning of her cheeks. She had known he was going to propose one of these Saturday evenings—she had been expecting it for several Saturdays now. But still she was not prepared to answer him. Still she did not know her own mind. Life, which used to be so simple, was now complicated.

Elmer was flustered too. He had memorized his speech

beforehand. It had been spoken tunelessly, by rote. She could tell he was nervous: he had cracked his knuckles all through dinner as he and her father talked about boring things like crop rotation and contour plowing and crop yields. She hated the sound. She would have been very bored had she not been so nervous. And after dinner, when her father dutifully left them alone in the parlor for a half hour or so, pretending he wanted to walk off his dinner even though he never ate much, Elmer finally proposed.

Above the sofa the old Seth Thomas clock ticked away the minutes. Her father would be back soon, elaborately rattling the screen door to announce his presence, coughing like a goat as he shuffled through the back of the house and into the parlor. She must say something before he returned.

"I must say this comes as a complete surprise to me, Elmer," she lied.

He looked at her circumspectly. "I hope I haven't been too bold. I thought . . . I thought my feelings were apparent some time ago. I reckon I thought wrong."

"Oh, no, I have been aware you were fond of me. I've been quite aware of that. But I wasn't sure you were thinking of marriage right now." Her voice fluttered and died. She was careful not to appear eager.

"I'm thirty-six years old, Miss Fannie. I've been ready to settle down for years. I'd of married sooner if it hadn't of been for Mom's lingering on so like she did. I couldn't ask anyone else to take care of her. She was a good woman, but she was unreasonable after Pop died and she took to the bed. I couldn't ask the likes of you to be a bride in a house of sickness." He paused. "But now she's gone, and the house is empty. A man can't work a farm and keep a house too. He shouldn't have to. I can't cook, can't sew. And I'm a lonely man, Miss Fannie." His pale blue eyes reached out and appealed to her. They were the same washed-out blue as his faded denim clothes. His voice was dry as a leaf of winter.

Dryness: that's what she thought of when she thought of Elmer, Fannie realized, watching him fold his huge dry hands across his middle as he awaited her reply. His hands were cracked and dry and his face was dry. The skin scaled in little flakes around his forehead, around his ears. That came from being out of doors so much, she supposed. Little dry grains like sand at the corners of his eyes. Even his speech was dry: laconic country syllables coming from somewhere in his head rather than from his throat. She supposed if she ever summoned nerve enough to reach out and stroke that lock of ash-colored hair that stubbornly fell across his eyes, it would be dead to the touch. The thought made her shiver. She clamped her hands firmly in her lap. She loved to stroke Homer Vincent's silky black hair, but she would never touch Elmer's. It would be dry as fodder.

Elmer cleared his throat again, making a grating sound. "You don't have to answer right off," he said, his voice and the ticking of the clock becoming one in her mind. "I know there are other considerations. I mean, that Vincent boy. Why don't you study it a spell? I don't mind. I can wait. I've been single all this time, a little longer won't do me no harm." He forced a smile and then looked at her out of the corner of his eye. He was hurt that she kept silent so long after he delivered his speech.

"I'll certainly consider it, Elmer. And I am ever so flattered you would ask."

He stood up, jamming those hands into the slit pockets of his trousers. "Don't be flattered. Nothing to be flattered about. I know I'm not the gayest blade to ever walk in Sussex County. I don't have style. But I'll take good care of you," he said, the voice becoming a mumble, a mere husk of a voice.

Beyond, in the kitchen, the screen door rattled ceremoniously and then her father's steps crossed the soft linoleum. Elmer planted his denim cap squarely on his head and started for the front door.

"Next Saturday night again, Miss Fannie?" It was a question.

"Yes. Of course. Come again at suppertime. Father has a nice big duck he's been saving for no good reason at all."

He ran his big rough tongue around his lips. "A nice big duck! I must admit I'm mighty partial to duck."

"Is that so?" she said vaguely.

"It is a fact. I'm mighty partial to duck. Take some people, they've got a powerful sweet tooth in their head. But not me. I'm a meat-and-potatoes man. And I'm mighty partial to duck," he repeated.

"Yes, well, we'll have something to look forward to then, won't we?"

"I presume." He stood awkwardly at the door, poised for flight back to his farm where, she supposed, he would feel free to take off his jacket and scratch himself wherever he happened to itch.

"Elmer?"

"Ma'am?"

"I'll have an answer for you on Saturday." She smiled at him encouragingly.

"That's a load off my mind! I thought for sure you was going to think on it for months maybe." His hand was on the doorknob, then he turned around. "Oh. I almost forgot. Here." He withdrew a twenty-dollar bill from his frayed black wallet and handed it to her. The bill, like the wallet, was wrinkled and ageless. "Would you be so kind as to deposit that in my account on Monday?"

It was the same question he put to her every Saturday, handing her a bill and waiting, sucking in his breath as if he expected her to refuse to perform the simple task. In the beginning he accompanied the request with an explanation: He only left the farm to come into town on Saturday, farmers' shopping day, and the bank was closed on Saturday. But after the first three or four deposits she made for him, he no longer felt it necessary to repeat the explanation, the justification, though he was always clearly embarrassed at the imposition he felt he was placing upon her. In truth, Fannie never minded the trips to the bank. They gave her an excuse for going downtown, where she liked to window-shop, to gaze at the pretty dresses and brand-new shoes in the windows of Birdie Pusey's store. Her father always was afraid she would spend money if she went downtown, and restricted her when she had no valid excuse for going.

Now Fannie's father was turning down the lights in the parlor; it was nine o'clock. As soon as Elmer left, Fannie and her father would retire for the night. The couple heard Fannie's father hugely yawn somewhere in the house. Elmer said good night, mounted the dilapidated wagon before the porch stoop, gave his drowsy mare a "Giddy-ap," and was gone. The wagon's raucous clatter and the horse's clopping on the cobbles dinned in Fannie's head long after Elmer was out of sight.

"Elmer asked me to marry him tonight," Fannie told her father as they ascended the narrow stairs, the light he carried throwing weird and contorted shadows upon the wall.

"It's about time," her father said. Fannie was twenty-two years old, on the very verge of spinsterhood. She supposed her father would rent out her room when she finally moved out. She liked that room, with its yellow and white striped wallpaper, its pine four-poster bed.

"What do you think I should tell him, Papa?"

"That," her father said formally, "is entirely up to the dictates of your heart."

The dictates of your heart? What did that really mean? Did it mean liking to stroke Homer's hair? Liking the way he smelled when he came to her right after he had shaved? Or did it mean the solid feeling she got whenever she sat next to Elmer? Elmer was a man, Homer was a boy.

" 'The heart has its reasons,' " her father quoted at the top of the stairs. " 'The heart has its reasons that reason does not

know.' I learned that at normal school, Fannie. Before I had
to quit and go to work. I could have learned more, if there had
been any money." It was cold upstairs. Fannie wanted to wrap
her arms about herself. Finally her father said, "Good night,
daughter," and left her alone.

He left her alone for days. Usually her father told her what
she must and must not do, but he remained silent on the topic
of Elmer Willms. She was certain her father wanted her to
marry as soon as possible, but he left the choice to her. She was
petrified with the magnitude of the consequences. All week her
hands were cold as ice, while her cheeks flushed with fire. She
must choose between Elmer and Homer Vincent, and she herself had promised to decide before Saturday night! It was impossible. They were so different; their lives were so different.
And her life would be so different, however she should choose.

Homer Vincent was handsome. She worried that perhaps he
was too handsome. She never knew what he did on Saturday
nights. Did he see lots of other girls? He said not. She reserved
Saturday night for Elmer, since that was his only day in town.
She saw Homer on Sunday, that wonderfully long day of the
week when her father always took a nap from right after
church until suppertime at four. In good weather Homer took
her canoeing on the millpond; the water sparkled and Homer
was good with a paddle. In bad weather they sat in the parlor
and played parcheesi. With Homer there were no awkward
silences as there were on Saturday nights with Elmer. With
Homer she was never aware of the passage of time. He was
lively, entertaining, and full of funny stories. If she married
him, she would have fun all the time.

Or would she? Homer was very poor. Except for his little
leaky canoe he didn't seem to own anything, not even a wagon
and mare as tired as Elmer's. Homer was a salesman in the No-
Credit Hardware Store. There was no money in clerking in a
store, but that didn't seem to bother him. He made very little
and spent what little he made. Homer lacked ambition, Fannie had decided with a sigh some weeks before. But he was

awfully handsome and quick. He had never asked her to marry him, but she knew he would. He said Mr. Small, his boss, had promised him a raise in salary in the autumn. Precious little that will amount to, Fannie had thought at the time. But now that raise loomed large in her mind, because she was sure once it was an actuality, Homer would propose.

"Fannie, have you decided what you'll tell Elmer?" her father asked on Wednesday evening, peering over the top of his newspaper to where she sat crocheting a doily.

"No." Her crocheting hook danced nervously beneath her fingers.

"Don't you think it's about time you decided?"

"I have until Saturday night," she said, gathering her doily and needles, leaving her father behind his paper. She scurried up to her room.

It was too early to sleep, so she decided to dust off her shoes. She took them from the closet. Fannie owned two pairs—an everyday pair and a Sunday pair. She picked up the everyday pair and fondled them close to her as she wiped them with a soft cloth. She loved shoes and took good care of them. Because she was so careful, they lasted longer, and she didn't have to ask her father for money for shoes so often. Whenever she asked for money, he looked into his checkbook and frowned. Ever since his first business venture as a young man had failed, he had pinched pennies; he pinched them even now when he did not have to. Her father had a system for shoes: whenever a pair of her Sunday shoes no longer looked good enough for Sunday, it became Fannie's everyday pair. Then she would buy a new Sunday pair, which in time became her everyday. Her father always inspected the Sunday pair before he would allow her to buy another.

Sitting on the floor of her room with a Sunday shoe in her lap, Fannie's mind drifted to the time when she had had no shoes of her own. That was when she was little, when her mother was still living and her father was poor. They were even poorer than Homer's family, who lived by the mill in a house that leaned. Her father had tried to run a regional wholesale grocery business, and the big outfits from Philadelphia and Wilmington had come in and ruined his trade. He had been left with a warehouse full of canned peas and corn and carrots and tomatoes. Her father had taken her into the warehouse the day before someone came and claimed the stock for debts. He showed her his shelves stacked to the ceiling with canned vegetables and told her he was very, very poor. She could not understand then how anyone could be poor and still own all those canned peas.

Yet they were so poor they had to move out of their house and into the country, where they lived in a shack on her mother's father's property. They lived there until her father began selling insurance and saved enough to move back into town, where they could hold up their heads once again. Fannie had hated those years in the country. She hated the cold drafty shack and the smell of the hogs. She hated walking four miles to school in the winter. But most of all she hated wearing her brother Ellwood's shoes. Because there was no money to replace the old ones she had outgrown, she had worn her dead brother Ellwood's shoes. The first day she walked to school in them they slipped on her heels and made blisters. When she clomped down the school corridor, the sound of them seemed to echo and bounce off the walls. Clomp, clomp. How she hated the sound of those too-big shoes! But it was not until she was called to the blackboard to do an arithmetic problem that the shoes were discovered. She tried to lift her feet daintily but the dreadful shoes went clomp! clomp! and one of the boys—Horace Radish it was, she would always remember who it was and hate him for it—Horace pointed at her feet and said for all the class to hear: "Look! Fannie's wearing *boy's* shoes!" Then everyone looked at her feet and laughed and laughed. She wanted to flee past the desks, out the door, and down the hall to the girls' washroom, but the shoes would have clomped and she might have stumbled. So she stood at the blackboard and wept while the entire class laughed at her shoes.

It was getting late. Fannie carefully placed the Sunday shoes in the closet next to the everyday shoes, and in performing that familiar ritual she made her decision. She would marry Elmer. Homer Vincent, for all his smiling and handsome ways, for all his marvelous stories and pretty palaver, would never have any money. He would never be able to give her lots of shoes. Elmer was frugal. Every week for months he had been salting away those twenty-dollar bills. His farm prospered. He must have been saving twenty dollars a week for years. Fifty-two times twenty, that's over a thousand dollars a year, saved, free and clear! The figures made her head spin. He was rich! He wore the same old denims and his wagon was rickety, but he was rich all the same. He was country, just as country as he could be, but he would be a good provider. She could learn to love him.

It was a simple wedding. Her father had looked into his checkbook, frowned, and told her she must have a small affair. It did not matter. She was to be through with his penny-pinching and delivered from a life of penury with Homer. She made her own gown, and she knew she looked pretty when she entered the parlor on her father's arm and was married to Elmer Willms before that selfsame sofa upon which he had courted her Saturday after Saturday. A small group of friends looked on. Homer Vincent sat in the corner, partially hidden by the potted fern. Fannie glanced his way several times during the ceremony, and he looked sad. His sadness was her sadness too, and finally she could not look upon him any longer. He appeared especially handsome, sulking behind the fern, and she saw that he had bought a new navy-blue suit just for the occasion. Elmer wore a clean pair of denims. She was ashamed he had not worn a suit. He seemed to buy nothing but denims. She would change that.

After the ceremony they climbed aboard Elmer's wagon and set out for the farm. She had never visited it. She knew where it was; she had once ridden by it on the way to a Sunday-school picnic, but she had never stopped. And it would not have been proper to go there after Elmer started courting her; his parents were dead, there were no chaperones on the farm. So all she knew of it was her recollection of tall poplar trees near the dirt drive and a pleasant-looking farmhouse painted white.

The poplars were blighted and the house was not very white, she noticed as the mare pulled them past the farmhouse and proceeded from habit toward the barn. Elmer pulled on the reins, forcing the mare to stop before the house so he could deposit his bride on the porch before unhitching the wagon in the barn. The house had once been whitewashed, but never painted. The porch boards sagged and sighed beneath her weight as she paced and awaited Elmer's return from the barn.

It did not take long to tour the house—there was little to see. You entered into the kitchen. The first thing Fannie looked for was an icebox; there was none. "Ice house is out back. Next to the privy," Elmer stated carefully.

The privy? No plumbing either? She was getting a headache. This was all too primitive for words. As Elmer led her into the only other room downstairs, the parlor that he called the "sitting room," Fannie resolved to convince him he must have proper plumbing installed. Even the ancient Romans had plumbing!

The sitting room was an embarrassment. It may have sufficed for Elmer and his invalid mother, but it unquestionably would not do for a couple of means who wished to entertain. And she did so much wish to entertain her friends from town. If she could only get to town once a week, she would have the town come to her. But the sitting room depressed her considerably, and she had not expected to get depressed on this of all days. Nevertheless, there it was: nothing but three wooden lawn chairs dragged indoors, painted bright green, and made to do. There were no curtains at the windows; the room had no cheer. Even her frugal father would think this room too scantily furnished.

That entire first week Fannie was depressed, and by midday

she always had a headache. She tried not to let Elmer discern her mood; she humored him, she submitted to him, she cooked the kind of country fare he liked. She learned to throw corn to the chickens and to find the eggs in the henhouse; she even pumped water twice a day for the hogs. And on Friday afternoon, standing at the pig trough, feebly priming the rusty old pump that coughed and wheezed, she realized how wretched she really was. The smell of sour swill and manure offended her nostrils. It seemed everywhere she stepped her feet sank into something soft and repulsive or live and crawling. She gazed at a huge bald squinty-eyed sow, a creature complacent in her rankness and covered with mud, and Fannie knew she had been foolish to think she could ever again live on a farm. Already she missed the window-shopping, the rattle of carriages going by her door, the peaceful strolls by the pond. Perhaps in time—in a year or so—she could persuade Elmer to get a tenant family to occupy the farm. Then they would move into town and live a proper life with proper plumbing. But until that time, she must make the best of things.

Making the best of things certainly called for improving the farmhouse; she couldn't live in it the way it was. She didn't want to overstep, but she must be firm. So at dinner, after Elmer had stomped into the house in filthy boots, after he began eating the grits and greens he had insisted she cook, Fannie looked up and said softly, "I'm going to fix up the sitting room."

Elmer kept shoveling the hominy down without missing a beat. He eats entirely too fast, she thought, and with his elbows all over the table top. Why hadn't she noticed that whenever he came to eat with her and her father?

"That's nice," he said, sopping up the juices on his plate with a piece of bread, wadding the bread into his mouth. "Real nice. What you going to do? Paint? I got some of that there green paint left over."

"I am not going to paint. I want to buy some decent chairs," she said. "Horsehair chairs. And a horsehair sofa. A coffee

table. Maybe a nice tea service. Lots of folks have got tea services. And I'm going to get some ferns and some flower stands to
set them on, and a carpet—"

Elmer stopped eating. He leaned forward and looked at her
squarely. He smells of perspiration, she thought distastefully.
Perspiration and horses and manure. He should bathe every
day, not just Saturday mornings. That's barbaric. She would
have to tell him so, but not tonight. Everything in good time.
There was so much to tell him. Suddenly she felt quite tired
and old beyond her years.

"Why are you staring at me?" she shrilled across the plank
table.

"Because."

"Because *why?*" Her voice was strident.

"Because I'm wondering just where you think you're going
to get the money from to buy all those fine and fancy things."
He wiped his mouth on his sleeve, ignoring the napkin set by
his plate.

"Why, from your savings account, I suppose. You've got it,
you may as well use it for the house. That's what savings are
for, isn't it? To get what you need when you couldn't ordinarily get it?"

"My savings account," he said softly, as if he liked the sound
of it. Then something happened that Fannie had never seen
before: Elmer laughed. He laughed and then let out a merry
whoop and slapped the table top so hard she was startled. The
slap sent the coffee sloshing over into the saucers.

"And what's so funny?" she asked, puzzled and hurt, watching the man she had married start to drink his spilled coffee
from the saucer, smiling all the while.

"Nothing," he said. "Nothing. 'Cept you can't get much fine
furniture for twenty dollars."

"Twenty dollars? Why twenty dollars? You save that much
every week!"

Elmer chuckled so hard he sounded like an old setting hen.

"We only got twenty dollars to our name. Not even that. I spent six on your wedding band. That there piece of gold wrapped around your finger."

"I don't understand." Her throat felt tight and her head pounded. "What about all those twenty-dollar bills I put in the bank every Monday?"

"I came into town and took them out every Friday. The same twenty-dollar bill, week after week." Now he tilted back in his chair and adopted a considering look. "Oh, they didn't give me back the *same* bill every week, I reckon. But the same amount. Twenty dollars deposited, twenty dollars withdrawn."

He got up from the chair and stretched. "I'm bushed. Going to turn in. You come on along." Then, as he left the kitchen, he said over his shoulder: "I had to do *something* to best that Vincent boy!"

Fannie sat at the table for a long time. Her husband was waiting upstairs. Even the way he made love was dry. Then, in the aching of her head, she heard the clop-clop of Elmer's mare, Elmer's worn-out mare clopping down the highway, bringing her to this farm, and the clop-clop of the mare was the hideous clop-clop of the secondhand shoes upon her feet not so long ago. *We are what we have been,* she thought. *We become what we were.* As she sat, the dark of night seemed to creep in through the windows, to enter the kitchen and wrap icy fingers around her bones. The mare went clop and the shoes went clop and finally she left the table and slowly climbed the stairs to the room above.

Songs of
Three
Seasons

It is Mother's Day. I stand in the choir loft and walk forward to the pulpit. I hear Mr. Hoffecker push a button on the console behind me, and the pipe organ begins to throb and hum. It makes the floor boards vibrate beneath my feet, like the Funny Feet machine on the boardwalk at Ocean City, the one you put a nickel in and it makes your tired feet feel good. Now the pipe organ squawks a peculiar liquid sound, a sound like somebody having an enema. Enemas are awful. Mother always wants to give them to me, and I try to act as if I don't mind.

I look out over the congregation. Everyone sits with his hands folded in his lap. Mr. Parkinson is snoring in the third row. He should be home in bed like Daddy. Daddy drank too much last night. I try not to think of Daddy. I see Allie's white hair and Mother's flowered hat bobbing in the rear of the church. It is the same hat she wore last Mother's Day. Only I didn't have a solo then. I hope Allie doesn't start making his awful noises and ruin my solo.

Mr. Hoffecker starts the introduction and I think back to last Wednesday night. I wasn't sure I'd have it until then. I held my breath when I heard old man Hoffecker say, "And now about the solo part—" He waited until the last possible rehearsal to assign the solo. I heard the other boys around me whisper and squirm in the loft. Some looked at me, I know, and some looked at Brandon Cooley. Brandon Cooley has a nice voice, but he doesn't sing as loud or clear as I do. When he sings, Mother says she can't hear him where she sits in the last pew. Brandon's voice is like he is, timid and thin. He's older than I am but my voice is bigger. That's why I have sung more solos than any other boy in the choir.

"It's a very difficult solo," I hear Mr. Hoffecker say in my mind. "Especially the transition in the middle—"

Mr. Hoffecker looked right at Brandon when he said it. I held my breath.

"I think Derald ought to get this one," Mr. Hoffecker said. I let go my breath like a balloon and smiled. I heard the older boys grumble. Some in the second tier, bigger boys than me, used to sing solos all the time until Minister Kling asked me to join the choir. Even though I was too young. Derald ought to get this one, Mr. Hoffecker said. Derald ought to. Derald, Derald, Derald. And I am only eleven years old.

Nothing can ruin Mother's Day for Mother now, I think. She will hear my solo and she will have her present. Which one will Daddy get? I wonder. When I gave him the money, those twelve quarters, I told him to get her either green stone earrings that sparkle or a pair of purple gloves. It didn't matter which. At the time I didn't know why I asked for those particular things. Then I remembered rich Mrs. Pettingill, who used to come to our house wearing those things when I was little. I still see her around town, but she never visits any more. It was because of Mrs. Pettingill I asked for green earrings or purple gloves. So Mother can look like Mrs. Pettingill.

"Where did you get this much money?" Daddy asked, weighing the stack of shiny quarters in his big hand. They made a bright sound when he closed his fist around them.

"I saved all my weekly allowances the past three months," I said, and it was true: no popsicles, no candy bars, no bottles of Royal Crown or Dr. Pepper. I saved my money for Mother's Day. The present was to be from both me and Allie. Allie only gets a dime a week and he always spends it the first day. He always buys a double-dipper ice-cream cone, week after week. He eats it so fast he gets a headache between the eyes and he still drips ice cream all over his hands no matter how fast he eats. He spends all his allowance, so I gave Daddy money for us both. That's all right. Allie isn't right in the head.

Friday night when Daddy came home from the factory, I ran to the front door. I had a plan: I'd take the present from him and run upstairs with it and hide it under my bed before Mother even saw it. Then she would be completely surprised on Sunday.

But Daddy had no box or bag. All afternoon in my mind's eye I had seen it: a stiff white box with bright-colored ribbon wrapped around it. Inside, the box would be stuffed with white tissue paper that crinkles when you touch it or even breathe on it. That was what the box would be like. But his hands were empty.

"Where is it?" I cried as he hung up his stiff old coat in the closet. The coat keeps his shape so that when he closes the door it is as if Daddy is hanging in the closet on a hook.

"Where is what?" He looked angry with me for asking.

"The present!" I whispered hoarsely, desperately trying to keep my voice out of Mother's range. She was in the kitchen, peeling potatoes for dinner, cutting out all the ugly little potato eyes, dropping them off the edge of her knife into the garbage pail.

"Oh, that," he said. Then he looked odd. "It slipped my mind, Derald. I guess I forgot."

I felt like crying, but of course I couldn't cry just then. I had to wait until later in my room. "How could you forget something as important as that?"

"I've got a lot more things on my mind than the foolishness you cook up!" he shouted. "Don't worry. I have to put in over-time tomorrow. I'll get something on my way home."

"Not just *something*. It's got to be either green earrings or purple gloves. I've told you that."

"What is it?" Mother asked from the kitchen. "What are you two going on about out there?"

"Nothing," my father said. I was afraid he would give away our secret, but he didn't. "I was just telling Derald that I have to work tomorrow."

"Oh, Clarence," she said. "It's the third Saturday in a row!"

"I'm not in much position to complain, am I? We need the money!" he roared. "For things like Derald's voice lessons, for example. Two dollars a lesson! That Mrs. Swensen makes more than President Truman does!"

Mother came to the doorway. She was framed in the arch as she said, "You should be ashamed of yourself, Clarence Per-kins. We should be willing to make sacrifices to develop Der-ald's talent. The boy has a real gift. Mrs. Swensen says he's her best pupil. And Mr. Hoffecker gives him all the solos at church. Of course, you wouldn't know about his church sing-ing, would you? You're always sleeping one off."

"Not *all* the solos, Mother," I said. "Just most of them." I meant it to sound humble, but it didn't come out that way.

"You're getting too big for your britches, boy," my father said. He narrowed his eyes and gave me a look that sent my gaze to the dim grapes on the wallpaper.

Saturday night I fought to keep awake. Long after Mother gave up waiting dinner for Daddy, long after the Seth Thomas clock struck midnight, I was still awake in bed, propped up with my pillows plumped behind me, waiting for his arrival. Beside me Allie had been asleep for hours. Some nights he rocks back and forth, back and forth in bed, rocking until he wears himself out, and then he can sleep. But tonight he went to sleep right away, and I lay there for hours, listening to the house settle, waiting. I should have remembered the other Saturdays Daddy worked overtime. He and his friends left the factory together and went somewhere to drink beer. He didn't return until late those nights either.

I must have dozed, because when I heard the front door, I jerked upright. I popped out of bed and ran to the head of the stairs. My father stood in the hallway below, carefully removing his heavy old coat. It seemed to take him a long time. He reached for a wire hanger, then dropped the hanger to the floor with a clatter. "Jesus Christ," I heard him mumble. He stooped and groped for it, and finally placed the coat in the closet. He walked toward the kitchen. I heard the refrigerator door open. He was going to eat. His hands had been empty. I had seen him the entire time—when he came in, when he took off his coat, when he hung it up. There had been no package.

I felt tears collect in the corners of my eyes. I ran back to bed and hid under the covers, muffling my sobs, trying not to wake Allie. I hid there until I heard Daddy slowly climb the stairs. I heard the heavy shoes drop to the floor from the bed, one thud after the other. The bed springs screeched as he crawled in. I lay under the tent of my blankets and wondered what I would do in the morning. It would have been easy for me to go downtown and buy the present myself. That is what I should have done. That is what I had done other years when Allie and I needed to buy a present. But this year I was so busy with choir practice and music lessons and homework, I had asked Daddy to do it. And he had said he would.

Suddenly I recalled the great pockets of his coat. That's where the present was! He had got it after all, and it was in one of his pockets! A pair of earrings, a pair of gloves, how much room could they take up? Whichever he bought, it would still be just a small package. Small enough to fit in a pocket. I slid my feet into my bedroom slippers and padded down the stairs to the hall closet. I pushed my hand inside the outermost pocket, trembling with excitement. The pocket still carried the cold of the out-of-doors. There was nothing in the pocket except the cold. Then I felt around and located the other pocket. *Let it be in there,* I prayed as I slowly inserted my hand. My fingers touched cardboard. A book of matches, old and wrinkled and used up. That was all.

It was Mother who heard me. It was she who rushed down the stairs and found me in the closet, beating at the coat with Allie's baseball bat. I struck the coat harder and harder. With each blow the bat made a hollow thud, the sound of Mother's wire rug beater against the living-room carpet strung up on the clothesline.

"Derald! What in the world?" She pulled the bat from my grasp.

I couldn't look at her. Then I said, "A bad dream. I was having a bad dream. I must have walked down here in my sleep." In many of the books I read people walked in their sleep, though no one in our family had ever done it.

She pushed the hair out of my eyes. "Poor dear. You're all keyed up over having to sing the solo tomorrow."

We sat in the kitchen and drank hot milk together. She crumbled toast in my milk and made me eat it. I didn't want to go to bed, because I didn't want Sunday ever to come.

But it came. I stand here, waiting to sing my solo. After church I shall tell my mother everything. About how she was supposed to have a present from me and Allie, a surprise that I would give her at the dinner table just before dessert. Now the stores are closed. I can give her nothing. The only thing I have to give is my voice. She loves my voice. I open my mouth and start to sing. I sing a golden gift of love.

I ring the bell and then walk right in. I used to wait for Mrs. Swensen to come and answer, but that was years ago. Now I

know that before my lesson she practices at the piano and
likes to stay there instead of getting up to come to the door. I
think she likes me to hear her playing. I ring to announce my
arrival and then enter the dark hall. Mrs. Swensen's house has
the longest, darkest hall I have ever been in. It is lined with
bookcases full of old leather-bound books and files of music.
When I was little, I was scared to be in that hall alone, it was so
dark, but now I linger each time I enter. I scan one or another
of the bookcases, my eyes adjusting to the dark, finding authors' and composers' names that excite me. Mrs. Swensen
lends me the books I mention I'd like to read. I take good
care of them, which isn't easy, living in the same room with
Allie. Allie tears things up. He nearly tore up Mrs. Swensen's
Carmen score. I caught him just in time.

"Derald? That is you, yes?" Mrs. Swensen calls out. She calls
that each time I enter, and it is always me. She has no other
pupil at four on Monday afternoon.

"It's me," I say. Today I decide I shall not ask about Dr.
Huptmann. The last time I asked if he had replied, her face
went red as a tomato and she began to shout: "Who does he
think he is to ignore me? I told him my credentials! He knows
I sang once with the Metropolitan. Does he think Olga Swensen cannot recognize talent when she sees it? Is that what Otto
Huptmann thinks?" I had been hurt and embarrassed by her
outburst: hurt that the choir director was not interested in me,
embarrassed that he was snubbing Mrs. Swensen. I swore not to
ask again. Five weeks was long enough for a reply. It was obvious now her letter would go unanswered.

I push through the heavy sliding doors to the room Mrs.
Swensen calls her studio. She is seated at the grand piano. A
vase of daffodils is on the piano today, the first flowers of
spring. When she sees me, she jumps up from the bench. She
begins waving a scrap of paper in my face.

"Derald, Derald, so look here! What do you think? A letter
from Otto Huptmann, yes? Yes! Otto Huptmann apologizes

for the delay in answering my letter. On account of being on tour with the choir, he says. Otto Huptmann will be delighted to audition you for the Capitol Boy Choir. How do you like that, Derald? You are happy, yes?"

I am so happy I don't know what to say.

"We must work, work, work! The choir sings in Wilmington on the twenty-ninth of next month. That leaves only five weeks to practice. You must practice like never before. Breathing, phrasing, everything. You must be in absolute top voice to audition before Otto Huptmann."

It had seemed that Huptmann would never answer; now everything seems to come too fast. How can I possibly be ready? What if he accepts me? What then? The choir has its own school. I will have to go away to the Boy Choir School. That means not having to look after Allie all the time. That would be good. But I'd never see Mother. Once or twice a year, maybe not that often. Mother is getting old. Even I can see that. Mother needs me.

"Do you know what this means, Derald? Such a musical education you'll receive. You'll work with Huptmann and his guest conductors. Go on tours, see the cities of the world! Do you know what an education that will be? Instead of this. Instead of Public Landing all your life!" She says the town's name with contempt.

"Oh, I'd never stay here all my *life*. Just as soon as I'm through high school I'll leave—"

"You'll leave this year. With the Capitol Boy Choir." She is determined.

"What if I'm not good enough? What if they turn me down?" I stand in the enormous room, illuminated by a flood of sunlight streaming through open casement windows, and I tremble with emotion.

"You are good enough. More than good enough. You not only have the voice, you have the training, if I do say so myself." She puffs up her enormous bosom like a pigeon. "You will show people what a good teacher Olga Swensen is. You, my best pupil. My *Wunderkind.*"

So I sit in the dark auditorium and roll and unroll sheets of music in my hands. The boys on the stage are arranged on pyramid-shaped platforms. When they open their mouths, they are angels. I have never heard such voices. The sopranos hit notes I know I have never reached.

"I can't do it," I whisper to Mrs. Swensen. "They're too good."

Even in the dark I can see her frown. "You're just as good. Better, even, than most. You have a great natural voice. Some of those boys, what voice do they have? Nothing, that's what. Little nothing voices. Huptmann built a voice for them. With you he doesn't have to build, it's there." She pats my hand. I stop toying with the music. She is right, I know. I do have a fine voice. And I am ready for the audition. I should sit back and enjoy the concert. I flatten the music across my lap and open my ears to the Bach chorale filling the auditorium. I have come to realize during the past month that this is the biggest opportunity of my life. My chance to leave behind this small town, the school where boys make fun of me for singing. I can go out into the big world, where I belong.

The curtain falls, the lights come on. Mrs. Swensen stands up and grabs my arm. "Come. We can't delay. Your coat! Don't leave your coat on the back of the chair!" Her voice verges on the hysterical. I realize she is more nervous than I. It is as if she is the one who will have to sing.

Backstage, choir boys rush around, some pulling off robes before they get to the dressing room. Beneath the robe each wears a suit. I have on a sport shirt and slacks. I am embarrassed I didn't wear a tie and jacket. What was I thinking of? Some of the boys look at me and I stare back, trying not to flinch beneath their gaze. I can't let them think I am afraid. Mrs. Swensen pushes me ahead of her, like a baby carriage. I want to pull away, to show the boys I don't need her to push me on the stage. I can go up there myself. I am ready.

Dr. Huptmann is at the piano. His back is to me but I know it is he. He is thin and wears a navy-blue suit. The back of his head is bald. I think to myself, I hope my hair never falls out. Daddy is bald. I don't want to look like Daddy. Daddy wants me to ask Dr. Huptmann how much the school costs even before I audition. Mrs. Swensen says that is a mistake. She says I should let Dr. Huptmann hear how good my voice is, and then let him know we're poor. He will want me in the choir so badly he will give me a scholarship then. That is what Mrs. Swensen says.

"Ah, Mrs. Swensen, is it?" Dr. Huptmann turns on the piano bench to face us. His eyes are bloodshot. He looks as if he needs a great deal more sleep. "Mrs. Swensen and her prodigy, is it?"

"I am Mrs. Swensen, yes. And this is my student, Derald Perkins."

I extend my hand. Dr. Huptmann takes it and gives it a slight shake. His hand is cold and moist. I look away from his big bloodshot eyes, sad as a basset hound's, and see that some of the boys are staying. They are not leaving the stage at all. They lean against the piano, waiting to hear what I sound like. They wait to hear me sing. I feel my throat go tight, as if someone is wrapping wire around it.

"You wish I should play for Derald, or you, Dr. Huptmann? We brought music. You see he is prepared. Palestrina, Praetorius, and some Grieg."

Dr. Huptmann pushes the music aside with a wave of his limp hand. "That won't be necessary, Mrs. Swensen. I prefer to give an audition of my own fashioning." His houndlike eyes search my face. "Are you ready to begin?"

I feel as if I cannot speak. If I open my mouth, nothing will come out but little mouse squeaks. But somehow I speak. My voice is fine. "Any time is all right with me."

"Good, good," Dr. Huptmann says. "First, the scales. All the scales." His long thin fingers run a scale. "Now, after me . . ." he instructs.

I sing the scale. The boys beside the piano look at one another and smile. Are they smiling because I am good or bad?

Dr. Huptmann runs the same scale again. "Once more," he says. I repeat it, thinking: If I go away, Mother will be alone. Allie is no company and my father goes off with his friends. She will be all alone in that house. My voice thins out toward the top of the scale and I wince. I have done it on purpose.

"That's all right, that's fine," Hound-eyes says encouragingly. He runs another scale, this one higher. My mind strains to determine how many keys he has skipped, how many pitches higher I must begin. Mrs. Swensen never skips around like that. Mrs. Swensen always takes the scales in sequence.

"Well?" Dr. Huptmann says, loooking at me. They are all looking at me.

I sing the scale, thinking: I will never see my mother again. On the seventh note I crack my voice again. So I won't have to leave Mother. Dr. Huptmann nods.

"He can do better!" Mrs. Swensen says anxiously. "Derald can do much better than that, can't you Derald?"

"Quiet!" Dr. Huptmann shouts. "I will have *quiet* when I audition!" Mrs. Swensen backs away from the piano. She stands some feet away and studies the laces on her sturdy oxfords.

"The last scale again, if you please." He runs the scale. I sing it. This time I crack my voice on the fifth or sixth note. The boys behind the piano nudge one another and smile. I cannot look at them. I look at Mrs. Swensen, who can keep silent no longer: "He is nervous. It is the nervousness." She rushes forward to the piano, clutching Dr. Huptmann's suit sleeve.

He pulls his arm free. "No, Mrs. Swensen, it is not nervousness." Then to me, "How old are you, boy?"

I clear my throat. "Twelve, sir, going on thirteen."

"Ah. There you have it," Huptmann says, closing the lid on the piano with a terrible thud of finality.

"There we have *what?*" Mrs. Swensen demands. Her face is tomato color again.

"It's very simple. The boy's voice is changing. A little earlier than with most boys, that's all." He starts across the stage.

Mrs. Swensen shouts after him. "Ridiculous! Never have I heard his voice is changing. Never! You think I would not know? I, who work with this voice every week?"

"Either you choose not to notice, which is likely, or it has just begun." His voice is full of contempt, as if he has been deceived. As if Mrs. Swensen has tried to play a trick on him. I feel sorry for Mrs. Swensen. It is I who am playing tricks.

"It never cracked like that before. Honest," I say to the back of his blue suit as it disappears behind the heavy velvet curtain. I try to sound disappointed.

"Tough luck, kid," a buck-toothed boy with freckles on his nose says. The choir boys file off the stage as if in a procession.

"Why didn't you tell me?" I said to Mrs. Swensen. "You should have told me my voice was changing."

"There was nothing to tell. Just tonight it begins. Perhaps," she says. There is tragedy in her voice. I do not look at her. I know that in her mind the cities of Europe are disappearing, the fancy private school, the public concerts, the adoring crowds. There are just the two of us left on the stage. Overhead, the lights are snapping off one by one. Now, I think, what will I tell Mother?

I don't care if it rains or freezes, so long as I've got my plastic Jesus on my dashboard! I sing with Bobby Vinton's voice coming through the TV tube. Our voices fill the empty Saturday afternoon. Christ, that boy can sing, I think, watching him gyrate on the screen. But he'd better watch out. Bobby Vinton, Frankie Randell, Chuck Jackson, Lenny Welch, Jerry Butler—the whole passel of them better watch out. There's going to be some real competition shortly.

I go to the refrigerator and take out another can of Bud. It hits the back of my throat cold.

"Another beer, Derald? It's not even five o'clock yet."

"Get off my back, Mother. I've got lots to think about."

"You're drinking too much lately, Derald. Just as soon as you get home from the factory you start in. And all day Saturday and Sunday. All you do is sit around and drink."

"Beer? You call that drinking?"

"I most certainly do. It's what sent your father to an early grave."

"I thought his nagging wife did that."

"Derald!" She starts to cry. I go over and put my arms around her. How many times have I put my arms around my mother in this stinking house?

"I'm sorry, Mother. I didn't mean it."

"I hope not," she sniffles. "It isn't like you. You don't sound like yourself lately, Derald. You're not the same Derald Perkins you used to be. It's all that rock and roll music. You never used to listen to that trash."

"It's not trash!" I shout. I realize my voice is too loud. I soften it. "It's what's happening today. Music of today for the people of today."

"You sound just like somebody on the television."

"I hope so. Because I'm going to be there someday. Someday soon. I want a slice of that great big pie. You think I'm going to sit around here and work in Accounts Receivable at the fertilizer factory all my life? Ha!"

"Well, I don't know why you've gone in for all that beatnik music. You used to sing such lovely songs. You were always so refined. Why did you stop going to Mrs. Swensen? She thought you were really going places. Now look at you. Those boots you wear. And your hair—it's longer than mine is!"

I pat my hair. "Yeah. Nice, isn't it? It's even longer than Monte Rock the Third's."

"You should wash it once in a while."

"Oh, Christ."

"I won't have that kind of language in my house!"

"Sorry."

"No you're not. You're not a bit sorry. You curse and drink beer and sit before that television all day long. What's going to become of you, Derald? You're twenty-six years old!"

"I'm going to become a big star. I'm going to become famous and make millions of dollars," I say flatly. "I'm going to become the nation's idol," I say, and smile. I grab my mother around the waist and start dancing her around the linoleum floor of the kitchen. Her apron strings swirl around us like banners. Suddenly she pulls away. Her face goes the color of flour.

"But what if it doesn't work out? What happens to you then? What happens to *us*, Derald?"

"Things will work out. You know they will. You've always said I was going to be famous. You're the one who taught me never to forget that. It's just taking longer than we thought, that's all."

She wipes her nose on her sleeve.

"You know I've written to Caly Cole and Soupy Sales and Ed Sullivan, lots of people. It's just a matter of time before one of them gives me a break. I'll go on Ed Sullivan's Show and knock 'em dead. Then I'll have it made."

Just as I say that, a loud *twang* comes from upstairs. I know what it is before I look. I go sick all over. My guts start crawling like snakes. *"Goddamn you,* Allie, leave that guitar alone!" I scream. I run up the stairs two at a time. When I reach the top, I'm out of breath. I'm not in such hot shape.

Allie is sitting in the middle of the bed with my guitar in his lap. He's drooling spit all down his chin, all over my new two-hundred-dollar guitar. His fat fingers tug at the strings like he's trying to pluck a chicken.

"Gimme that thing!" I yank it from him and he starts to cry. I take out my handkerchief and wipe the slobber off the wood. I keep my Gibson nice and clean.

Allie keeps crying. He sits in the bed, his eyes blank as egg cups and these big tears run down his cheeks. It makes me want to vomit, seeing my stupid brother sprawled out on the bed in filthy undershorts, needing a shave and going bald, crying because I won't let him ruin my new guitar.

I go to the stairwell and yell down to Mother. "I'll tell you what *I'm* going to do!" I holler. She comes to the bottom of the stairs and I see her framed there in the shadows of late afternoon. "As soon as I cut my first record and make a pile, I'm sending Allie away to someplace where I don't have to look at him! I'm sick of looking at him! He's going away to some fancy hospital where they get paid to put up with him!"

"Oh, Derald," my mother whispers below.

"And I'll tell you something else. We're getting rid of this chicken-shit house. I'm sick of looking at this wallpaper, listening to that goddamn clock, smelling my father in every room ten years after he's dead—"

"You're drunk, Derald," my mother says, and turns to go.

"I am not drunk, I'm not, I'm not," I say. Then I see how my mother's shoulders sag, how thin and tired she looks, how her step falters. I start slowly down the stairs, my beer belly bobbing before me like a woman great with child. "Where do you want to live after we leave Public Landing, Mother? New York? Paris? Hollywood?"

The Death of a Good Man

The others remarked on the depth of her grief, but she did not care. Let them talk. Let them look at her. Sarah McCormack sat and openly wept on the porch of a second-rate hotel in Ocean City, Maryland, conscious of the stares of the middle-aged and elderly ladies on either side of her. These women all had hair either the color of rat fur or the color of laundry bluing. They whispered about her and their phlegmy voices mingled with the whispering of the sea breeze. Their infernal rocking in creaking wicker chairs and the rocking of the waves on the beach below dizzied her. She tried to stop mourning but she could not. She had been in this hotel for several weeks and every day she cried.

She usually was composed in the mornings, waking alone in the rude room on the fourth floor. And she was all right in the shower, going through her ablutions by rote. But as soon as she

entered the faded grandeur of the fern-lined dining room, and
the heads of all the ladies turned toward her—away from fly-
specked menus and identical pink celluloid rosebuds set in
identical green crackle-glass vases on separate tables—she felt
the tears well up. She could not keep them back.

"Come, come, my dear," one of the women on the porch said
to her, taking Sarah's hand from where it rested on the arm of
the wicker rocker. "You must pull yourself together. How long
ago did he pass away?" Everyone in the small hotel knew she
was recently widowed.

"Three weeks," Sarah said, unable to control the waver in
her voice. She sniffed the salt air and pushed her glasses higher
on the bridge of her nose. Lately her glasses were forever sliding down her nose.

"Well, now, time heals all wounds," the older woman said
sweetly. "I know. I went through it myself." She smelled just
like all the hotel's old women, a musky odor compounded of
perspiration mingled with talcum powder. "Time heals all
wounds," the woman said again, and patted Sarah's hand with
her own liver-spotted paw.

Sarah heard, but she did not think the platitudinous words
would ever have meaning for her. She pulled free of the
woman's grasp, stood up, and purposefully walked toward the
hotel's front door like an old horse making for the stable.

The day he died was an ordinary day. At the breakfast table
he read a prayer out loud from the *Daily Word*. Then she put
in her hours at the office, performing her clerical job efficiently
and energetically. No one could organize hundreds of accounts-
receivable billings in a metal tub as fast as she. She called Leslie twice, once in the morning and once in the afternoon. She
had spent the lunch hour shopping for a new pair of bedroom
slippers for him. His old maroon pair of Daniel Greenes finally
had worn out completely, the stitching unraveling at the heel,
the gray felt lining balling up beneath his feet. After work she

picked up several days' groceries, then stopped at the Spirits Shoppe and bought him a new fifth of Cutty Sark. (Once she had made the mistake of buying him J&B instead; the price was the same, and she thought he might welcome variety. But that was before they had been married very long, before she knew how well he knew his own mind.)

As she came down the apartment-house corridor with her packages, she heard the familiar sound of his television and smiled. When she entered the apartment, he was just as she knew he would be, sprawled out on his Barkalounger chair, his short legs wide apart, chewing on a black cigar and watching the Braves play the Yankees. She made a ceremonious protest about the cigar smoke and fanned the air over her head. He laughed and raised his head for a kiss. She kissed him full on the lips.

"I bought you some more Scotch," she said. She was proud of the way she remembered all his needs. "And a new pair of bedroom slippers! How do you like that! Now, just you give me those old things this very minute—" He laughed again and watched the television while she playfully tugged at the old slippers until she had one in each hand. She carried them outside to the incinerator chute. They smelled of feet but it was a good smell, a husbandly smell. She lingered a moment before dropping them down the chute.

Then she set about making dinner. She had to be careful of his diet. They ate very simple fare now. Anything heavy or spicy or the slightest bit exotic gave him terrible heartburn and indigestion. He would roll and writhe half the night on the twin bed next to hers. The matter of planning menus was one of the few instances when she was aware of the twenty-five years that separated them. It was then she realized that, despite appearances, by the calendar he was an old man.

She started dinner simmering and then came over to his chair and settled like a cat in his lap. "How was your day, darling?" she asked.

"Oh, all right, I guess. The dry-cleaning man came at eleven and dropped off some things. I had the man at the garage grease the car." He studied the tip of the dark cigar in his hand, not touching her at all. "And right after lunch I called Hackensack and checked up on Uncle Leopold. Poor old guy, I guess he's just about holding his own, and that's all." He replaced the cigar in his mouth and his gaze returned to the television screen. His teeth bit down on the soggy cigar. They were his own teeth, all of them, and they both were proud of that.

"I do hope he shakes that pneumonia soon," she murmured, pressing her head against Leslie's broad shoulder. He was wearing the plaid Pendleton shirt she had given him the Christmas before, a bright orange and green plaid. "At his age pneumonia could be . . . could be fatal," she said. She never liked to talk of death around Leslie, although he was always very philosophical about it. "When I die," he had once lectured her, "the Little Man Upstairs will take care of me. Just put your faith in the Little Man Upstairs."

"Yeah, yeah, well, Uncle Leopold is a tough little guy. He'll pull through it," Leslie was now saying. "He's had a lot worse than pneumonia, and he's still alive and kicking. I do think I'll drive over to see him on Sunday though."

"You do that. I'll get caught up on the housework around here. I'm afraid it's been neglected this week. I've just been so beat lately, filing all day—" She got up and carried his ashtray to the garbage pail and emptied it. She put the coffee water on to heat. In the tiny kitchenette oven the chicken was cooking and spitting fat. On the burner peas bubbled and trembled.

Sarah never went with him on those Sunday pilgrimages to the old people's home in Hackensack. She always invented an excuse. She was certain the place would depress her terribly. She hated to see people who had given up living; old people just using up their allotted days, their skin gone gray and scaly, their eyes filmed over like a hen's. Why did people allow themselves to get that way? Look at Leslie: even at his age he was pretty trim, vigorous. He did sit-ups most mornings. He sat under the sun lamp when there weren't any ball games on the television. And every Saturday morning she helped him put a weak blond rinse in his hair so it didn't look all gray. Even in his seventies he managed to look not much older than she. When they went to Lake Mahopac for two weeks at Skippy's Cabins the first part of every July, he put on a bathing suit and went on the beach with everyone else. His body was a good body still. His legs were thin and very short, but he had a powerful trunk.

As she dropped a pad of butter into the pan of peas, Sarah's thoughts projected to the summer that stretched ahead, those two precious weeks when she got him out of the apartment and away from the city. How she looked forward to those two weeks! Every July she bought a different doll as a souvenir of Mahopac. The china dolls lined her dressing table, each bearing a different year painted on its skirt. When they had first been married, they used to go out to dinner once or twice a week—to a little Chinese restaurant he liked, the Grand View, which actually had no view at all, only a brick wall—and sometimes took in a movie at Radio City Music Hall or the Roxy. But that had been years ago. Now he liked to stay in, surrounded by the morning and afternoon papers, his cigars, his coffee in the morning and Scotch in the evening. And always the television droned and flickered before him. On Saturdays she did the shopping, rinsed his hair, occasionally gave herself a perm, and then in late afternoon pulled her chair beside his and watched whatever he was watching. On Sundays she always did the cleaning while he charitably drove across the river to Hackensack to cheer Uncle Leopold. Sarah missed Leslie terribly the few hours they were apart every Sunday and she sat by the door awaiting his return like a newly weaned puppy.

"It's about time to write Skippy again," she announced from the kitchenette.

He looked up and his face brightened. His eyes could be the brightest blue she had ever seen. They were blue as the sky over Mahopac where children laughed and splashed. She loved children.

"Yeah, be sure and tell the little guy we want the same room again. The one we've always had."

"He'll save it for us, I'm sure," she said. "He ought to know by now."

She lit the two scented candles and they sat down to dinner. This was the hour she liked best of all, the hour she worked and lived for. An overwhelming sense of well-being overcame her. Across the table Leslie said grace; he had always been a religious man, though they never went to church. As he unfolded his linen napkin with his long graceful fingers and placed it across his lap, she marvelled at the grace with which he performed the ritualistic gesture: he looked like a priest preparing for the Eucharist. Leslie McCormack had style; he always had had it. It was this sense of style that had attracted her to him more than his undeniable good looks. And as his looks diminished, the style remained, became refined, triumphing over the encroachments of age.

His style caused other members of her family to talk, to say stupid and cruel things about him. Her sister Maybelle was jealous of her for catching a man with such obvious looks and such style. Maybelle had always been jealous of her because Sarah was the pretty one. Her mother and Maybelle had told her Leslie would make her miserable, that he was too old for her, and that she would be chained to a decrepit old man most of her years. They said he was just looking for someone to wait on him hand and foot in his old age. They kept saying that phrase, "hand and foot," over and over again. But they weren't content to stop there. They said a friend of a friend of the family knew all about him, that he had been a bounder in his day. After that she did not speak to her mother and Maybelle for a dozen years. She married Leslie McCormack the first time he asked her and she guessed she had shown them. She had made the best of all possible marriages. The only regret she had was children: she had agreed with him before they married that there should be none.

What really burned her mother and Maybelle, of course, was that she hadn't married Harry Peterson. If she had, she and all the rest of the family would be well off. Before she died her mother used to keep sending Sarah newspaper clippings about Harry Peterson or about the Peterson Paste and Glue Company. At first Sarah would feel a faint stirring in her bowels or wherever when she read about him. Now she didn't feel the slightest twinge. She was not cut out to be any Mrs. Harry Peterson. She wouldn't even know how to act at those fancy dinner parties he and his wife were always giving! No, she was meant to be Mrs. Leslie McCormack.

"Where's the gravy, hon?" Leslie was pushing the mashed potatoes around on his plate with his fork.

"There isn't any. I mean, I broiled the chicken this time. It all dripped away."

"I see. Oh, all right." He looked disappointed. She was always disappointing him in some little way. She must remember always to make him gravy in the future.

Only there was no future. As she sat delicately carving slivers of white meat off the chicken breasts for the two of them, Leslie gave out a little grunt. His hand darted up to his chest as if he were about to give the Pledge of Allegiance. And that was all. One grunt, one movement of the hand, and he slowly tipped forward, nose first, like one of those hollow plastic ducks that perch on the edge of water glasses and bob their bills back and forth into the water. As she watched, Leslie tipped forward like a duck. His face came to rest in the mashed potatoes.

Between then and the funeral two days later Sarah somehow did not shed a tear. She was accepting the fact of his death in a way she thought she never could. Being twenty-five years his junior, she had always known she would outlive him: his death simply came some ten years before she supposed it would. She was consolable. He had been a good man, he had led a good and full life. He had had his religion and would be saved. And their marriage had given meaning to her existence, had given her a center about which to revolve. How could you cry for the quick and apparently effortless death of an old man? An inner voice told Sarah that it was meant to be this way. She was glad for the years they had had together.

Maybelle told her how brave she was. Maybelle had come up all the way from Public Landing for the funeral. She stayed at the hotel down the street from Sarah. Probably because she did not want to have to sleep in a dead man's bed, Sarah thought grimly. There was Leslie's bed unused; it was stupid for Maybelle to spend good money on a hotel room. Sarah was not going to let herself be silly about such things as his empty bed. She found herself putting away the unopened bottle of Scotch and the unworn bedroom slippers. Someday soon she would return them to their respective stores. The day after he died she threw out all his unsmoked cigars. She would dispose of his clothes later, all those beautiful clothes she had picked out herself.

"It really is remarkable," Maybelle said again. "I don't know how you do it. Not a tear! If anything happened to my Clovis or any of the children, I'd just die." Maybelle had four children—three girls and a boy. Every time Sarah saw them she could not keep her hands off them. They were so beautiful.

"There's really nothing to cry about," Sarah said simply, straightening the seams of her black mesh hose and tugging down the girdle that kept rising beneath her dress. "I can't cry when we were so happy together for so long. Over eighteen years! Death must come to everyone, sometime. To you, Maybelle, and to me too."

"It's remarkable all the same," Maybelle said again. Sarah thought if she said the word one more time she would scream. "I must say, Sarah, that I . . . well, I don't quite know how to say it . . ."

"Go on. What is it?" Sarah was lowering a simple black straw hat on her head like a crown. She had bought no new clothes for the funeral. She had long ago stopped buying gay dresses in bright colors. Her wardrobe consisted entirely of sensible black and navy blue; she had no difficulty assembling suitable widow's weeds.

"I just wanted to say how sorry I am I said all those bad things about Les. Before you got married, I mean. I had him figured all wrong. . . ."

"Hush," Sarah said, and smiled forgiveness on her sister like a queen. "What's forgotten is forgotten." She led Maybelle down to the street and flagged a cab. One would have thought Maybelle was the wife of the deceased, the way Sarah took the lead. Oh, she had become efficient, she had. All these years of living in the city had taught her how to survive.

What was left of the family was seated on folding chairs in the funeral parlor when Sarah arrived with Maybelle. It was one of New York's largest funeral parlors—Sarah was sparing no expense, spending nearly all of Leslie's relatively modest insurance policy on his funeral—and as soon as she stepped into the room she knew she had made a mistake: the place was too big. She should have chosen a smaller concern with a smaller parlor. Here the few mourners were lost in one corner of the long rectangular room: her Aunt Gertrude from the Bronx; Leslie's fat sister Hazel and her husband Raymond, who flew down from Canada; Sarah's young nephew Stephen, who worked on Madison Avenue, and his wife, who wore too much make-up and looked like a clown; they were all bunched together, up front. Separated from the family by a respectful distance of two rows was a handful of girls from Sarah's office, secretaries and clerks who had never even met Leslie. And that was all. The only other person she might have marshaled into making an appearance was Leslie's uncle Leopold, who obviously was now too sick to make the trip. She had toyed with the idea of calling the home in Hackensack when Leslie died, but the news alone might have killed the old man. She would get word to him at some later time.

Looking at the meager crowd, Sarah felt a kind of fury rise up within her: Why couldn't there be more? Gangsters always had huge funerals, gangsters and phony movie stars. Why not one for a really good man like her Leslie? Then she calmed herself. He had not worked for years. And they had not socialized. He didn't like having other couples over to the apartment. They had had no friends, only each other. That had been enough.

Leslie was laid out at the head of the room. Sarah walked quite briskly down the long row of empty wooden chairs and approached the coffin, conscious of the eyes of others upon her. She studied his head carefully where it was propped like an overgrown doll's on a fleecy white pillow. He looked good. In death the slack muscles around his mouth and eyes had grown taut. Beneath the high dress collar of his shirt you could not see the flesh of his neck, which in life had sagged like sad turkey wattles. He looked years younger now, as he had looked when she had first met him and fallen in love. His hair was combed and brushed and looked especially blond under the severe spotlight. Sarah smiled and was glad she had rinsed his hair for him just the Saturday before.

She stood before the coffin for what seemed a long time. It was copper, heavy and gleaming and expensive. Then an organ she could not see began to play. The music slid sonorously from note to note. She took in the music and inhaled deeply the scent of the flowers banking the coffin. She had sent most of the flowers herself, sprays of red roses. Then she bent over and, before the rest of the family and onlookers, she gave Leslie McCormack the last kiss she would give him on this earth. His lips were cold as porcelain.

She rose awkwardly from kneeling by the coffin and turned to face the gathering. For a moment she wobbled on her heels. Then she was aware someone was approaching down the long empty aisle. Was it the minister come to conduct the service? Sarah could not see well without her glasses. Years of filing accounts receivable had robbed her of good distance vision. Then she could see it was not a man at all, but a woman in black, wearing a veil. Sarah knew she was a stranger. She was pleased to see someone else had come to join the mourners, someone other than family and girls from her office. Now the group would not look so pitifully small.

"So nice of you to come," Sarah murmured softly, extending her gloved hand to the woman. The woman took it. Who was she? Sarah wondered. Someone who had known Leslie before they were ever married? Perhaps she was just another of those women who are professional funeral-goers, women with empty lives who have nothing to do but troop around to every funeral they see listed in the newspapers.

The woman retained Sarah's hand and gazed, for the briefest of moments, at the form in the coffin beyond. Then she let go and turned to leave.

"Oh, can't you stay? For the service?" Sarah said softly. She was determined to fill the first two rows of chairs at least.

"No," the woman said, still moving away. She seemed to glide.

The others were staring at them now, watching with more than polite interest. Still Sarah pursued the woman. "I'd like to record everyone present in the guest book," she said breathlessly. "What is your name? I'd like to write it down."

"Just say an old friend," the woman said. Her voice was deep and husky, the kind of voice Sarah always associated with women like Marlene Dietrich. "I knew him longer than anyone," the woman volunteered. "Longer than you." Again she turned to go.

"Your name. Please, give me your name." Sarah was excited now. She felt her hands perspiring inside her dark gloves.

The woman lifted her black veil and looked Sarah squarely in the eye. The face was ageless. "Uncle Leopold," she said in a terrible voice. "I was his Uncle Leopold." Then, in a taffeta rush of black, she was gone.

"Who was it? Who?" Sarah heard Maybelle asking. "Who *was* that woman?"

And that was when Sarah began to mourn. Great tears streamed down her cheeks as she began to mourn. And it was Sarah she was mourning for.

The Angel of the Church

The illuminated angel can be seen for miles around. People as far away as Hebron say they can see it on clear nights. People approaching Public Landing on the state highway can see it, miles away, before any of the buildings in the town come into view.

The steeple of the True Vine Baptist Church had already been the tallest structure in the town, and when Mrs. Fulton Oldfield proposed that a huge, illuminated angel be mounted upon its peak, the church deacons were, by and large, quite pleased. The angel would make the church nearly a skyscraper. And it would give the Methodists in their squat cement-block church across the street a thing or two to contemplate. All the Methodists had was a pitiful cross perched upon their steeple, a tacky little thing made of nothing but wood. Mrs. Oldfield had originally contemplated giving the Baptists a cross—

bigger than that of the Methodists, naturally—but ultimately decided an angel was grander and more appropriate.

The angel was made to order by some firm up North and transported to Public Landing in a huge truck, guy wires carefully holding it rigid during the bumpy journey. It was made of heavy frosted glass, with electric wires transversing the inside of its angelic anatomy. The expression on its face was said to be serene, though, once it was mounted, no one could really see its features, it stood so high. And one has to say "it," because no one could tell whether the angel was a woman or a man, its hair being long but its body being quite stocky. Around its head bloomed a nimbus big around as a cartwheel.

Contrary to earlier rumors, the angel was not lighted with neon. Some of the Methodists had remarked snidely that the Baptists were going to erect a neon angel in memory of Fulton Oldfield; the Methodists thought a neon angel would look cheap. Several even suggested that property values in the block immediately would go down. But when the angel arrived and was laboriously raised to its place by a pair of professional steeple jacks (who charged an unheard-of twenty-five dollars an hour!), it did not look cheap. The angel generated a pure white light, pristine and cool in the evening sky. Mrs. Oldfield was gratified, the Baptists were pleased, and the Methodists had little more to say.

When Jim Passwaters first saw it, during the dedication service at which Mrs. Oldfield pressed the button in the church foyer that threw the angel into glorious blaze for the first time, he too was gratified. Fulton Oldfield's death had depressed him greatly. He had come home from the city for the service, and he would travel back a more lonely being. Mr. Oldfield had been an important influence upon Jim when he was a youth. He had spent many hours with Fulton Oldfield in the old man's dark house on Sycamore Street, and Oldfield's passing wrenched him: among other things, it meant he was no longer a boy. The angel was a tribute to an honorable and simple man who had been Jim's only remaining tie to a town he had outgrown.

Oldfield had been a scholar of sorts. At least his upstairs den was lined with books bound in dark leather and buckrum. When Mr. Oldfield had taught his Sunday-school class, years ago, Jim Passwaters had been in the class, and he was drawn to the man's ability to tell tales. That was before the old man's gums had become so sunken, before his hands had acquired their terrible tremor. Jim Passwaters sat in the group of young boys circling Fulton Oldfield and was entranced by the imagination that made old Bible stories live.

One day Jim asked Mr. Oldfield if he could borrow a book, and a long fellowship of book-borrowings and discussions followed. Nearly every week Jim would borrow several from the old man's den. He began by taking religious books, but the old man discerned that the boy had a desire for adventure stories, and soon Jim was borrowing volumes of all kinds. He never returned a book until he had read it from cover to cover; then Mr. Oldfield would question him on the contents. Sometimes they would mildly argue a point. They enjoyed themselves.

Jim Passwaters visited the old man and devoured musty-covered books because he had few friends. He was, to begin with, too quick for his classmates. In school he solved arithmetic problems in his head before the other students could solve them on paper. He read the newspaper daily and asked too many questions in current events class. And in the English course he was the only pupil in the room who professed to like poetry. He had always been a reader, and his classmates never forgave him that. When he was only twelve, he had been sick for months, and that was when he had discovered Dickens. After reading *David Copperfield* and *Oliver Twist,* he had sent his sister to the municipal library for more. He lamented that they had only *A Christmas Carol,* with sentimental color illustrations. He did not discover *Great Expectations* and the others until his fingers found them on Fulton Oldfield's bookshelves.

If the man gave him nothing else, he gave him Dickens.

It was Jim's somewhat frail nature that led him to withdraw into the world of books. Jim's sister was too old to play with when he was growing up, and he was younger than the other children on his block. He was ill-coordinated, wretchedly so, and at school, when the recess teams chose sides, Jim was always taken last. His name would finally be called with the greatest reluctance, accompanied by loud groans from the side on which he was to play and jeers from the opposition. At night he dreamed of himself standing there on the playground, the sole pupil yet to be chosen, while his contemporaries glared at him and shouted. In his dreams and on the field he always struck out. The only time he had hit a ball at all, that one beautifully sweet moment of achievement, the ball had miraculously landed right in the glove of the man on first base.

He tried to make friends, but it didn't work. He even tried to strike up a friendship with Robin Winslow. Robin took piano lessons each week, and Jim thought the two of them might be able to talk. Robin was a tall, good-looking boy who was considered peculiar. Once Jim had been walking down East Street and had seen Robin parading around the Winslows' littered front lawn, dressed like a woman. He had on one of his mother's old faded ball gowns, mauve-colored with scarlet-red lace. Robin had painted his lips into a cupid's bow with scarlet lipstick, and long rhinestone earrings bobbed below his lobes. Robin beckoned to Jim to come into his empty house to play, but Jim refused. Robin had the kind of face a guy always wanted to punch.

So Jim Passwaters had been driven to old man Oldfield's den. He felt at home there. Oldfield was a wise man. By profession he had been a clothier and in his earlier days he was a great joiner of clubs. He especially had enjoyed being a member of the Red Men, a local fraternal order whose initiation ceremony was said to be especially secret and frightening. On the wall of his den Mr. Oldfield had hung aging group photographs of the Red Men's members taken during successive years. He could tick off the names of all of them, many long since dead. He called each group "splendid chaps." Jim and Oldfield would sit in that den afternoons, after school was over, the sun's dying rays slanting through the window, and they would discuss the Red Men and books and religion. Mr. Oldfield had finally given up his Sunday-school class because of age or some other failure of the flesh, and he was eager for an audience. When he really wanted to punctuate a point, he would poke a palsied finger into Jim's chest.

Jim wanted to be a writer. When he was very young, he once wrote a short story about a stallion. He bound the loose sheets with a plain ribbon and called the book "Black Satin, a Horse Story." In high school he was writing nearly every weekend after he finished his homework. Some of the stories he took to Mr. Oldfield. His high-school English teacher was a young and inadequate woman, newly graduated from the state normal school. In class she openly flirted with the football players, especially Jake Semple, who was heavily muscled and had a car of his own. After nearly two school years of such behavior she was fired when Mrs. Semple lodged a formal complaint with the school board that the woman was molesting her son and damaging his health. Those two years did not do much to help Jim Passwaters with his writing. Miss Catherine Fletcher, his teacher in the junior and senior years, was much better, but always wanted to stick to the textbook before her. She thought discussion of any book other than the text was an extracurricular activity.

But Mr. Oldfield had read widely and his suggestions were sometimes helpful. He admitted that once he himself had wanted to write. He urged Jim to go to college and take all the courses in English he could. "Read the great ones, Jim. All the great ones. Then you'll know what it's all about. Not until." The two of them would discuss Jim's crude poems and stories over tea served nicely by Mrs. Oldfield in flowered cups.

Mrs. Clara Oldfield was a ghost of a woman, silently gliding around the downstairs of the house, waiting on her sick husband, boiling tea, arranging the *National Geographics* in their rack. She rarely spoke, and never intruded upon her husband and his company in the den unless he called to her from the top of the stairs for more tea, or for a pill to "ease the misery" in his sunken chest. The most anyone ever heard Clara Oldfield speak was the night she plunked down the artist's drawing of the memorial angel before the deacons. That night her eyes were bright, almost defiant, and she spoke rapidly and distinctly in defense of her project: Fulton Oldfield had taught Sunday school in the True Vine Baptist Church for nearly forty years. A memorial should be put up, and she had the money. Once the angel was affixed on the steeple and provisions made for its lighting each night, once the bronze plaque memorializing his name was bolted into the wall, Clara Oldfield scuttled back to her house, where she silently creeps about even to this day, dusting her husband's books and photographs of the fraternal order of Red Men.

During his earliest days of college Jim Passwaters forgot Fulton Oldfield. He had been awarded a full scholarship to attend a university in the North. There were those in the town who thought he was putting on airs, going to school so far away from home. It was as if the state university were not good enough for him, they said. Others thought he was being particularly disloyal to his heritage: both his parents were from the South, and his father had gone to a Southern school. But from the beginning Jim Passwaters yearned to go north—he was running as far away from his home town as he could. He had heard that people in the North, rather than ridiculing knowledge and talent, respected them. Once his bus arrived in the college town, he was a bird released from its cage. He boldly asked for directions to the college, and then hurried up the shaded avenue through a shower of golden leaves toward the lights ahead. His battered Gladstone bag awkwardly banged against his thigh, he was wearing clothes bought at an Army-Navy store, but suddenly all his timidity had vanished. He was free.

After he had been at college nearly a semester, a letter appeared in his mailbox when he had expected none. The shaky handwriting on the envelope was unfamiliar. In his room he tore the heavy, cream-colored envelope open and a letter from Mr. Fulton Oldfield dropped to his lap. It was a lively letter, for an old man. The former clothier chastised him for not having written his "oldest friend" (in terms of years), and begged him to visit on Sycamore Street during the approaching Christmas vacation. Jim's friend, perhaps his only friend in Public Landing, had not forgotten him. Jim was moved. When he boarded the first of several buses that made connections for his long journey home, he had in his bag a Modern Library edition of Plato's *Dialogues* to give to Mr. Oldfield, a duplicate of the first book he had bought at the college book store earlier that year. During the next four years, Jim visited Oldfield every time he went home. Eventually he found he was able to hold his own in literary discussions with his elder. He had performed well in his English courses. Once he discovered the Jacobean dramatists, he memorized whole passages, especially from his favorite, Webster. That writer's violence somehow satisfied his own vivid imagination.

After graduation he refused to return to Public Landing— the town and his family had nothing to offer him. Instead, he found a job on the second most-read newspaper in Philadelphia. But he disliked newspaper work from the first, and he felt he was writing short, simple sentences for short, simple people. He didn't know what he wanted to do for a career, but he was sure newspaper writing was not the answer. He had considered teaching, but thought he lacked the nerve to stand before a classroom day after day. So he rewrote obituaries and want ads and lived at the Y.M.C.A., carefully avoiding the other men who lived there. Several were obviously homosexual; others merely wanted to monopolize his spare time to assuage their own loneliness. One young man followed him out of the shower and dripped water all the way down the hall to his room. Jim had had to fight the naked boy to keep him out. The boy had pleaded to Jim to let him in "just for the night." Jim was repelled by the deviates and misfits in the building. But the rent was cheap.

He stayed with the newspaper for a little over a year. Then he drifted into another job, this one in public relations. It was even more distasteful. Once or twice he returned to Public Landing but it depressed him terribly. Most of his classmates, those who had been so popular in high school, had now settled down to isolated, humdrum existences as parents of passels of moon-faced children. Some lived in trailers on their parents' property; others bought small development homes near the canning factory. There was nothing whatever to do in the town. Aside from seeing his parents and his youngest sister, still unmarried and with a hair wart developing on her chin, there was no one to see. And his family didn't understand him or his way of life, his fruitless search for self-expression. "Why don't you come back home, James Lee?" they chanted. "Why don't you come back home? Why, you could edit the *Southeast Breeze* right here in Public Landing? We always thought someday you'd come back home and write for the local newspaper. . . ."

No, there was no one to see except, occasionally, Fulton Oldfield, now grown feeble and dim. On Jim's most recent visit the old man had confused him with someone else. Jim's trip south for the dedication of the angel in the old man's memory would be, he felt, his last.

It was years later, on a rainy Friday night in Philadelphia, that Jim recognized Robin Winslow across the room, in a restaurant in which Jim was having a solitary burger and beer, following a long day of trying to write advertisements for a new type of septic tank. He had left public relations for another unsatisfactory job, this time in advertising. Jim was sure it was Robin across the room, though it had been over ten years since he had last seen him. Yes, it was Robin, though his hair was much blonder. He held forth in a corner booth with a group of men younger than he. Jim watched him for a while, like a figure in a motion picture, someone at once removed from himself, yet somehow fascinating, as Robin flailed his arms and spoke in a raucous voice that carried across the sawdust floor and over the heads of all the beer drinkers in the darkened room. Jim had heard rumors of Robin's activities. In letters while at college and in conversations at home, he had learned that Robin had left Public Landing immediately after graduation, as if he too could not break away fast enough. Philadelphia had always been his goal, Wilmington being too small and New York too big. Like Jim, he was still having a difficult time finding himself. He had left Public Landing intent upon being a male nurse. He had enrolled in a hospital program, but for some reason had left. Then he had tried to become an actor. In high school he had been a member of the Thespians, and had reveled in costume drama. (All those sequins and feathers!) But his talents were not sufficient to satisfy Philadelphia casting directors. Jim remembered that now he was playing piano in cocktail lounges, where he was said to have quite a following. His picture had appeared in the *Southeast Breeze* the year before. It was a picture of Robin seated at a grand piano painted white, a mirror above the keyboard reflecting long, tapered fingers wearing many rings. He wore a bow tie and a sickly grin. The editor had run the picture and story about Robin's night-club appearances on the social page. His mother, a faded beauty now beaten by the world and working at the fertilizer factory, took time off from work to puff her way up the Big Hill to give the editor a piece of her mind for not running the picture on page one where, in the opinion of all her friends at the factory, it clearly belonged.

Jim finally caught Robin's eye. Robin threw up his arms in an extravagant gesture of recognition. He bustled to Jim's table and seized Jim's right hand and pumped it up and down. His grip made Jim feel as if he had immersed his hand in a jar of mayonnaise.

"Jimmy-boy! Jimmy Passwaters! What in hell are ya doing here?"

"Working. I work right around the corner, at the Fleck Agency."

"You *do?*" the voice soared. "Really? It's a small world. I work just a couple of blocks away. At the Pink Flamingo! I'm the star attraction, I'll have you know."

"So I read in the paper. The Public Landing paper, I mean. I didn't know where the place was, though."

"Well, now you know. You really must come over and hear me play. They say I'm real good. Really they do. As a matter of fact, John Beamly wrote me up real big in his 'Night Life' column in the *Bulletin*. Real big . . ." He busied himself unfolding a yellowed newspaper clipping that he extracted from his wallet like a prophylactic. The clipping consisted of a few comments about the piano playing of a new up-and-coming entertainer "not to be missed," currently appearing at Joe and Ida's Pink Flamingo.

Jim gave a little whistle of mock admiration and watched Robin carefully refold the clipping with satisfaction.

"So what do you do for kicks these days, Jimmy?" It was the first time anyone had called him that in years. Robin took the chair across the table. Jim's hamburger was getting cold, but he had not been hungry when he came in. He should spend some time with Robin. For all his ways, perhaps they could finally become friends.

"Not much. I try to write when I can."

"You mean, like writing books?"

"Someday I hope to write books. Right now all I seem to write is checks."

"And isn't *that* the truth? I'm telling you, this town is murder. A body can hardly afford to make ends meet, even when there's money to be had. And there *is* money to be had!"

"I suppose so. Not in writing, I'm afraid."

"Oh, there could be. I mean, couldn't there? What do you want to write about? Your old home town? Boy, isn't *that* a laugh."

"There's a lot could be written about. The people, I mean."

"People? In Public Landing? There's not a soul there I'd walk across the street to see."

"It's not all that bad, Robin. You know it isn't. But I never go home any more myself. Not since Mr. Oldfield died. I used to see him sometimes."

"Yeah, so did I. Wasn't he a corker?" A strange smile crossed Robin's face as he watched Jim set down his mug of beer.

"You used to visit Mr. Oldfield too?"

"Hell, yes. Half the boys in town did, one time or another. You knew that much, didn't you?" Robin lit a cigarette and blew a smoke ring into the air between them. It floated gently and circled Jim's head in the dim light, where it hung in time and space.

"Can't say as I did. What did you talk about, books?"

Robin had inhaled and now he pretended to choke on the smoke. *"Books?"* he cried, little tears of mirth starting down his lean, sun-lamped face. "Books? I don't reckon we talked about *books*. I don't reckon we *talked* about much of anything. When old man Oldfield had it in his mind he wanted some fun, he just called up one of us boys, and those of us with any sense came a-running. Hell, it was never less than a dollar he'd give us, sometimes more. Besides, all you had to do was stand there, for God's sake."

Jim sat looking at Robin and heard the words, words drifting across the table like the smoke reaching up to his head, his brain, and for a moment he forgot himself. He and the old man were sitting on the lumpy sofa in the den, a pile of books between them, two cups of tea steaming on the table.

"You're lying, Robin Winslow."

"Honey, I'm not lying. Why would I lie about a thing like that? I mean, I don't have to lie. Mr. Fulton Oldfield was the biggest faggot Public Landing ever did see. Even when he used to work in his clothing store downtown, he'd *always* want to fit you for a pair of slacks. He was glad enough to do *that*. He'd jam that old tape measure right up your crotch. And always managed to pop into the dressing room with another bathing suit just when you had your pants down. All the boys were wise to him. You couldn't help but be. Mercy."

Jim sat and watched the blasphemer move his lips. Robin looked like a fish he had seen in the aquarium, its mouth opening and closing like a bellows, yet making no sound, giving no meaning. Jim was beginning to think all of life was summarized in that silently flapping fish-mouth.

"The funniest thing was that wife of his," Robin was saying. *"She* knew what was going on all the time. I swear she did. One of us boys would ring the doorbell, and she'd let us in without so much as a word. And we'd go up the stairs where he was waiting in his bathrobe, and she never said a word. She never set foot upstairs until after she heard the front door close again, if then. There's a marriage for you. Why, a couple of times she even called me up herself when he was pretty sick. 'Mr. Oldfield would enjoy your company after school, if you'd care to stop by,' she'd say, without so much as a catch in her voice. 'Mr. Oldfield would enjoy your company.' I'll say he would. Dirty old man with his shaky old hands smelling of Vicks salve—"

Jim left the restaurant and went out into the Philadelphia night. Inside it had been smoky, and his eyes smarted. He walked back to his cluttered Y.M.C.A. room and for a long time looked out the window at the city lights. Outside his door he could hear the giggles of men cruising the halls.

The Lost
and the
Found

It was misplaced. Paul looked everywhere, in all the cartons marked PAUL'S ROOM in black crayon, emptying toys, clothes, and picture books in a huge pile in the middle of the strange new bedroom. When he had emptied the last carton and examined the mound of possessions several times, he left the room and began searching the cartons marked KITCHEN, LIVING ROOM, and MASTER BEDROOM.

"What is it, Paul? What are you looking for?" his mother asked, leaning heavily on her cane. She faced the window, her back to all their unplaced furniture, staring down at the city streets many stories below. When their trip was finally over and his father had stopped the car before this building and pointed up twenty stories and told them this was where they were going to live, Paul had not understood. With her bad leg, how could Mama get up and down so many stairs every time she wanted to go out or come in? That was before Paul learned about elevators. The elevator hurled them upward ever so fast, them and all these cartons the hairy, stinking moving men had packed but left for them to unpack.

"My lambie," he said, not looking up at his mother, but continuing to pick through the carton of kitchen utensils—a colander, bent pots and pans, a black skillet still shiny from grease, lots of ugly tin things.

"Well, it's not in *there*," she said. "Have you looked all through the boxes in your room?"

"I looked. It's not there."

"Daddy will find it for you when he gets back from the store. It's bound to be stuck away somewhere. Just be patient. You're so impatient, Paul."

He looked around the empty room. The walls were white as a refrigerator and still smelled of paint. "There's no window seat in my room," he pouted. "I used to like to sit in the window seat and look out at the squirrels and the leaves. . . ."

His mother's face looked sad. Finally she said, "A lot of things are different now, Paul. You'll just have to get used to things as they are. Daddy's company sent him here, and we go where Daddy goes."

"Why? Why couldn't you and me stay back in Public Landing?"

"Paul!" Her voice cut through him, then it softened. "You'll like it fine here after a time. I'm sure you'll meet some lovely friends at school."

He didn't want to think about school. That was two days away. He sat down before another packed box and began spilling its contents on the bare floor. This one seemed full of wooden coat hangers and shoes and shoe trees and pairs of his father's socks rolled into tight black balls. He knew his lambie wasn't in this box either, but he pawed through to the bottom anyhow.

Paul heard a key scratching at the lock, and then his father let himself in. They had never locked their house in Public Landing—no one there did—but here his father had locked and unlocked the door both times he went out to move the car and buy some groceries. "Everyone okay?" his father asked, crossing the room with a heavy paper bag. He went to the kitchen and began unloading cans and jars and fresh vegetables on the bare counter top. Paul's mother had told him it was time he started helping his father around the house, but he made no offer to help him now.

"Paul can't seem to find his lamb," his mother said. "Do you remember packing it, Earl?"

His father stood still in the kitchen for a moment, then resumed putting away the groceries. "Can't say that I do. But that was his job. He put out all his things that were to be packed, didn't he?"

"That's right, Paul. Do you remember where you put it last?"

"On the bed," he said. "It was on the bed with lots of things. My toys."

"Well, it'll probably turn up then. Don't look so glum," his father said, and laughed a strange laugh Paul had never heard before. His father looked at Paul's mother and then back at Paul. "Aren't you a little old for that sort of thing anyhow?"

"It's my lambie," was all Paul could say. He didn't want to wait to eat before unpacking the rest of the boxes, but his mother insisted. They downed a quick, simple meal that his father cooked before discovering what Paul had feared since afternoon: the lamb was nowhere to be found. He didn't cry or throw a tantrum. He put himself quietly to bed, not even waiting for sheets to be put over the rough striped mattress, simply falling on the bed and pulling his familiar red blanket with the frayed ribbon binding up and over him. It was the first time he had gone to bed without his lambie since he could remember, and it took him a long time to fall asleep. In the next room he could hear his parents moving around and talking. Once his father raised his voice and said, "Well, what if I did? It was long past time," and his mother said, "But Earl, you had no right—"

From the streets below came sounds of traffic, late into the night.

"Let's us have a look around this city of ours, Paul," his father said at breakfast. Paul could see his father had worked a long time during the night, maybe not even going to bed. Chairs were now placed, lamps were centered on tables, and all the cardboard cartons were gone. Only Paul's room remained to be put in order.

"I don't know," Paul said.

"It's Saturday, Paul. Why don't you go out and get some fresh air? See your new neighborhood?" His mother already looked tired, though it was the first thing in the morning. Maybe she wanted to rest, so Paul agreed to go.

The air didn't smell very fresh, and there was nothing of a neighborhood to see—just one tall building after another, with narrow alleys in between. There were noises that hurt his ears—sirens, jackhammers, horns—and everything looked dirty. Even the drooping flowers in front of their building were covered with a thick layer of black dust. He picked a few to take to his mother, but when he saw how filthy they were, he threw them away.

"Can we go back in now?" he asked after what seemed like a long time.

"We've just come out!" his father exclaimed. "Come on around here. In back of our building. There's something I want to show you." His father led him to the lot behind the apartment house. "This is one of the reasons I picked this neighborhood, Paul. For you." His father pointed. Paul saw a small cement plot with a seesaw, a set of swings, a sliding board, a jungle gym, and a basketball net hung hopelessly high above his head. One little girl was swinging herself on the creaking chain swing. That was all.

"I'll bet lots of boys play here on weekends and in the summer!" his father said enthusiastically. "Do you want me to leave you here for a while? You can find your way back in, can't you?"

Paul looked at the strange girl swinging back and forth. The girl looked at Paul too. When Paul's father's head was turned, she stuck out her tongue.

"No, I don't want to stay," Paul told his father, ignoring the girl. "I want to fix up my room so I can play there."

His father was disappointed. "You don't want to swing or anything?"

"I want to go to my room."

He stayed in his room most of the weekend. He arranged his toys and folded his clothes and took out the empty cartons. Through it all he kept expecting the lost lamb to appear beneath a jacket or a blanket or—miraculously—in a drawer or under the bed. On Sunday night he took the last empty carton out through the hallway, to the dark hot room his father called the incinerator. When Paul returned to the apartment after discarding the box, he knew he would never again have his lambie. That admission, plus premonitions of his first day at the new school the next morning, kept him awake long after he heard his parents climb into their bed.

The school was ugly and his teacher was ugly. She was a fat woman with a face round as the moon, and her black eyebrows grew together in one curvy line so they looked like one long fat hairy caterpillar on her forehead.

"What's your name, boy?" she asked him when he came in.

"Paul Toadvine," he said, and everyone in the room laughed. What was wrong with the name Paul Toadvine? No one had laughed at it before, in Public Landing.

This school was different from the one he had been in before. For one thing, here there were both colored and white boys and girls. And the bathroom wasn't in the clasroom.

When you had to go, you held up your hand and asked the teacher for a pass to let you leave the room. This was explained to him very carefully the first thing in the morning, but Paul waited until nearly noon before he held up his hand. He was timid and he didn't want to call attention to himself. Besides, if he wet himself, he could tell his mother it was the new teacher's fault: she was so mean she wouldn't let him leave the room to pee. His mother would feel sorry for him then. But the other pupils had already laughed at him once, and he couldn't bear that again. Finally, when he could stand it no longer, when he felt as if he would have to dance out of the room, he raised his hand.

The pass was a smooth piece of wood, like a shingle, and the word PASS was painted on it. As he carried it down the hall toward the Boys' Room, he approached another boy who had just been. The boy carried his pass before him like a sign, and with his hand he had completely covered the letter P. As they passed each other in the hall, the boy pointed to the three letters remaining visible and laughed out loud. Paul laughed too, to be polite. He didn't think it was so funny. He had heard that word before, but he had to go so badly, he didn't have time to think about it now.

The door to the Boys' Room was heavy. It took both hands to open it. When Paul stepped inside the smelly room, he saw three older boys leaning against the wall in the corner. They were smoking cigarettes. Paul was shocked. He thought only grown people smoked. People like his daddy. It made his daddy's teeth yellow and his breath bad.

Paul lay the pass on top of the porcelain latrine and hurriedly unzipped himself. It wasn't a moment too soon. What if he had wet his pants? What would the caterpillar-faced teacher say? What would his daddy say when he heard? Paul would have to sit in class all day with hot wet pants sticking to his legs, and they would smell and itch, and all the other boys and girls would laugh at him again. He was glad he had decided to raise his hand after all.

After he relieved himself, Paul shook his little organ vigorously, as his mommy had told him always to do. As he was shaking it, he heard a loud snicker from the corner where the boys were.

"What you doing there, Half-pint?" one of them called out.

Half-pint? No one ever called him that before. "Shaking the dewdrop off the lily," he said by rote. That was what his mother always called the tidy ritual.

Their loud guffaws echoed through the empty tiled room. "The dewdrop off the lily?" they howled. They slapped one another on the shoulder and laughed until tears rolled down their cheeks.

"Some lily," one said. He was the tallest, and had a dirty Band-aid stuck on his cheek. He kept narrowing his eyes so he would look even meaner.

"Shit, that boy don't know his ass from a hole in the ground," the second said.

"Or his cock from a water lily!" the third offered, and then they all three laughed even louder.

Paul zipped himself up efficiently, flushed the latrine, and walked over to the basin to wash his hands. He wanted to run out, to leave the three boys behind, but he knew he must always wash the germs from his hands.

"What do you think that thing is for anyhow?" the shortest one asked him, the one with long dark hair that hung straight over his left eye.

Paul started washing his hands without answering.

"I asked you a question, Half-pint. What do you think that thing of yours is for?" The three bigger boys had circled him where he stood by the sink.

"To pee with," he whispered finally, hoping that would satisfy them and they would let him go.

"Shit," the middle one said, the only one who had looked friendly before. "Shit." He stubbed out his cigarette on the black and white tile floor with a tennis-shoed foot.

"Sure, that's all it's for," the tall one said, narrowing his eyes even smaller. "And babies are dropped down the chimney by the stork. Right?"

"No," Paul said, glad that for once he had the right answer. "The doctor brings them in his big black bag."

He never knew three boys could make so much noise. Their laughs echoed and echoed above the toilet stalls.

"Listen, Half-pint," the short one said, giving his head a fancy toss so the hank of hair flipped out of his eye. "That thing is to stick into a girl good and hard, and when you do, it makes a baby. Everybody knows that. Where've you been all your life?"

It was the meanest thing Paul had ever heard. "Don't kid me," he said. "I know all about it. I'm in the third grade. Besides, I've got to get back."

The three pressed close to him now, hemming him in. He felt the cold porcelain of the washbasin against the small of his back. For the first time since he had come into the Boys' Room, he was really frightened.

"Who's kidding, Shithead?" the short one said. "Don't get wise with me."

"That's what it's for, kid. Everybody does it. Everybody that's *old* enough, that is. Like us," the tall one said, narrowing his eyes and looking at his companions for approval.

"Yeah," the other two said.

"I don't believe it," Paul said.

"Ask your old man. He'll tell you!" the medium-height one said. "How do you think you got born, Half-pint? Your old man shoved it up your old lady, and bingo!"

"That's a lie!" Paul screamed. "That's a dirty, rotten, filthy, stinking lie!"

"No shit," the short one said. "Not only that, but they enjoyed it! Your old lady got a real bang out of it."

"You lie, lie, lie!" Paul started hitting at them with his little fists, striking out in any direction. They started to fend him off, but he made so much noise screaming at them that they quickly left, afraid a teacher would come in and catch them. They left the smell of their cigarettes and the filth of their lies hanging in the air behind them.

Paul didn't return to the classroom. That was where his coat was, where his new books were. Instead, he walked down the three flights of iron steps and out to the city street. His father had walked him to the school that morning. It wasn't far from what they now called home. He could find the way.

His mother let him in when he buzzed. He had no key, wouldn't know how to use it if he did. In his mother's lap was a paper bag full of string beans she had been snapping, just like in the country.

"Paul? You're home so early. Is anything—Paul, you've been crying!" She didn't seem to notice he had left his jacket at school, for which he was thankful. He rushed past her and ran to his room.

He heard her limping heavily. "Paul, what's this all about? Something went wrong at school?"

"They said awful things about you and Daddy."

"Who did?" Her eyes went big with concern.

"Some boys at school. Big boys. Lots bigger than me."

She ran a cool hand across his forehead. "And what did they say? It couldn't be important. They don't even know us yet."

So he told her what they had said, every word just as they had said it. Her face got red and she stopped stroking his brow. She clasped her hands tight before her in her lap. "I'm sorry you were subjected to such *filth*," she cried. "I can't understand boys whose minds are in the gutter like that. They must be hoodlums or delinquents or something, to tell you things like that."

"Then it's not true?"

She paused for only a moment. "Of course not, Paul."

"And the doctor brought me in a big black bag?"

"Just like all babies come," she said, and he knew it was so.

He did not run into those three boys the next day, it was such a big school. His mother wrote a note to the teacher and put it in a sealed envelope. Paul held it up to the light in his room but couldn't read what she had written. He wanted to know what she had said. After the teacher read it, she didn't punish him for not returning to the classroom after visiting the Boys' Room. She smiled at him weakly and told him he was going to have to make some adjustments, he was getting to be a big boy now. He didn't know what "adjustments" were, but he agreed he would have to make some. She told him a teacher couldn't protect him every step of the way, and he said "Yes, ma'am," politely.

The following week Paul awoke late one night to the sound of thunder crashing around him. He had never lived in a tall building before. Would lightning hit their building and burn them all up? Thunder rolled in the distance. Electric streaks tore up the sky. If he had his lambie, he wouldn't be so scared. If he had his lambie, he could hug it tight and talk to it. Instead, all Paul could do now was wrap his arms about himself and hug his own thin body. That's what he was doing when the especially loud clap of thunder and extra-bright lightning seemed to hit the roof just overhead. Wherever, it was too loud and bright and it sent Paul tearing out of his bed.

He ran into his parents' room without knocking and was about to clamber into bed with them when he noticed their funny noises. His father was wheezing like the dry pump on the farm. Paul stood silently in the room and the next flash of lighting illuminated the bed and his father's terrible form where it was perched above his mother's, rhythmically pumping. In one crazy lightning-filled, tear-spilling instant Paul leaped on his father's back and started beating him as hard as he could. *You!* he cried. *You! It's all your fault! She had to lie to me. You do this to her like the boys said. You do it and that's why she's crippled!* He kept pounding and screaming until somehow his father led him back to his room and his mother pleaded with him to understand everything was all right; but he knew now that nothing would ever be right again.

Breakfast was something no one wanted to get up for. It was another Saturday in the city, and Paul stayed in his bed a long while, his parents in theirs. Finally they all got up and ate. Paul couldn't look them in the face and no one had anything to say. He finished his oatmeal and returned to his room. He thumbed through old picture books without looking at them. His father went out.

When the mother-killer returned, he was carrying a big white box tied with a blue ribbon. He stopped before Paul's door and rapped with his bony knuckles on the frame, though the door was wide open. "Can I come in, Paul?"

"Sure." He didn't look up at the mother-killer standing there.

"Paul, about last night . . . that's something you shouldn't think about or worry about just now. Later, when you're older, you'll understand it all. Okay?"

"Okay," Paul said to the mother-killer.

"Good. Here's something your mother and I want you to have. Sort of a present from us."

"It's not my birthday." He still didn't look up.

"Hey . . . since when do you have to have a birthday to get a present from your folks?" The mother-killer tried to laugh, but Paul didn't laugh with him. He'd never laugh with him again. Soon the mother-killer left Paul to open his package alone.

It was a stuffed lamb. Not like his lambie, exactly—this one was bigger, the fleece was rougher, and it had a stupid expression on its face. Paul's lambie had looked sweet, but this one was stupid. He tossed the plaything in the corner. Later, when his father went out for the paper and his mother was preparing dinner, Paul slipped out of the apartment with the lamb. He carried it to the incinerator at the end of the hall, pulled open the big black chute, and sent the lamb sliding down to the fiery destruction that waited below.

A Teacher's Rewards

"What'd you say your name was?" the old lady asked uncertainly, peering through the screen door to where he stood on the dark porch beyond.

"Raybe. Raybe Simpson. You taught me in the third grade, remember?"

"Simpson . . . Simpson. Yes, I suppose so," she said vaguely. Her hand remained firm on the latch.

"Of course you do. I was the little boy with white hair. I sat right in the front row. You always used to rap my knuckles with your ruler, remember?"

"Oh, I rapped a lot of knuckles in my time. Boys will be boys. Still, the white hair, the front row. . ." Her voice trailed off as she made an almost audible effort to engage the ancient machinery of her memory.

"Sure you remember," he said coaxingly. " 'Miss Scofield

never forgets a name.' That's what all the older kids told us. That's what all the other teachers said. 'Miss Scofield never forgets a name.' "

"Of course she doesn't. I never forgot a pupil's name in forty-eight years of teaching. Come right in." She ceremoniously unlatched the screen door and swung it wide for him to enter. The rusty spring creaked as the door opened and closed.

"I can't stay long, like I say. I was just in town for the day and thought I'd look you up. You were such a good teacher and all. I've never forgotten what you did for me."

"Well, now, I consider that right kindly of you." She looked him up and down through wire-rimmed spectacles. "Just when was it I taught you?"

"Nineteen thirty-eight. Out to the old school."

"Ah, yes. The old school. A pity about that fire."

"I heard something about it burning down. But I've been away. When was the fire?"

"Oh, years ago. A year or two before I retired. I just couldn't teach in the new brick schoolhouse they built after that. Something about the place. Too cold, too bright. And the classroom was so long. A body couldn't hardly see from one end of it to the other. . . ." She made a helpless little gesture with her hand. He watched the hand in its motion: tiny, fragile, transparent, a network of blue veins clearly running beneath the surface; the skin hung in wrinkles like wet crepe paper.

"That's rough. But you must have been about ready to retire by then anyhow, weren't you?"

Her watery blue eyes snapped. "I should say not. All my life I've had a real calling for teaching. A real calling. I always said I would teach until I dropped in my tracks. It's such a rewarding field. A teacher gets her rewards in something other than money. . . . It was just that new red-brick schoolhouse. The lights were too bright, new-fangled fluorescent lights, bright yellow. And the room was too long. . . ." Her gaze dared him to contradict her.

"I don't think much of these modern buildings you see all around either."

"Boxes," she said firmly.

"Come again?"

"Boxes. Nothing but boxes, that's all they are. I don't know what we're coming to, I declare. Well now, Mister—?"

"Simpson. Mister Simpson. But you can call me Raybe, like you always did."

"Yes. Raybe. That's a nice name. Somehow it has an honest sound to it. Really, the things people name their children these days. Do you know, the last year I taught, I had a student named Crystal. A little girl named Crystal. Why not name her Silverware, or China? And a boy named Jet. That was his first name. Jet. Or was it Astronaut? I don't know. Whatever it was, it was terrible."

"Sounds terrible," he said unenthusiastically. Then a shaft of silence fell between them. At last she smiled, as if to herself, and said cheerily, "I was just fixing to have some tea before you happened by. Would you like some nice hot tea?"

"Well, I wasn't fixing to stay long, like I said." He shuffled his feet to and fro.

"It'll only take a second. The kettle's been on all this time."

She seemed to have her heart set upon a cup of tea, and he was not one to disappoint. "Okay. If you're having some, I'll have some too."

"Good. Do you take lemon or cream?"

"Neither. Actually, I don't drink much tea. I'll just try it plain. With some sugar. I've got a sweet tooth."

"A sweet tooth, have you? Let me see. Is that one of the things I remember about you? Raybe Simpson, a sweet tooth? No, I don't think so. One of the boys I had always used to eat candy bars right in class. The minute my back was turned at the blackboard he'd sneak another candy bar out of his desk and start to chew away. But that wasn't you, was it?"

"No, it wasn't."

"I didn't think it was you," she said quickly. She was getting down two dainty cups with pink roses painted on them. She put them on a tin tray and placed a sugar bowl between them. The bowl was cracked down the middle and had been taped with yellowed Scotch tape. When the tea finally was ready, they adjourned to the living room.

"Well, how've you been, Miss Scofield?" he asked.

"Can't complain, except for a little arthritis in my hands. Can't complain."

"Good." He glanced around. "Nice place you got here." He took a sip of the tea, found it bitter, and added two more heaping spoons of sugar.

"Well, it's small, of course, but it serves me." She settled back in her rocker.

"You still Miss Scofield?"

"How's that?" She leaned forward on her chair as if to position her ear closer to the source.

"I said, your name is still Miss Scofield? You never got married or anything?"

"Mercy, no. I've always been an unclaimed blessing. That's what I've always called myself. An unclaimed blessing." She smiled sweetly.

"You still live alone, I take it."

"Yes, indeed. I did have a cat. A greedy old alley cat named Tom. But he died. Overeating did it, I think. Ate me out of house and home, pretty near."

"You don't say."

"Oh, yes, indeed. He'd eat anything. Belly got big as a basketball, nearabout. He was good company though. Sometimes I miss old Tom."

"I should think so." An old-fashioned clock chimed overhead.

"What business did you say you're in, Mr. Simp . . . Raybe?"

"I didn't say."

"That's right, you didn't say. Well, just what is it?"

"Right now I'm unemployed."

She set her teacup upon a lace doily on the table top and made a little face of disapproval. "I see. How do you get along?"

"Oh, I manage one way or the other. I've been pretty well taken care of these last ten years or so. I been away."

"You're living with your folks? Is that it?" Encouragement bloomed on her cheeks.

"My folks are dead. They were dead when I was your student. I lived with an aunt. She's dead now too."

"Oh, I'm sorry. I don't think I realized at the time—"

"No, I don't think you did. . . . That's all right, Miss Scofield. You had a lot of students to look after."

"Yes, but still and all, it's unlike me not to have remembered or known that one of my boys was an *orphan*. You don't mind if I use that word, do you, Mr. . . . Raybe? Lots of people are sensitive about words."

"I don't mind. I'm not sensitive."

"No, I should think not. You're certainly a big boy now. And what happened to all that hair?" Looking at his bald head, she laughed a laugh as scattered as buckshot. "My, you must be hot in that jacket. Why don't you take it off? It looks very heavy."

"I'll keep it on, iffen you don't mind."

"Don't mind a bit, so long's you're comfortable."

"I'm just fine."

She began to rock in her chair and looked around the meager room to check its presentability to unexpected company.

"Well, now, what do you remember about our year together that I may have forgotten? Were you in Jay McMaster's class? Jay was a lovely boy. Always so polite. You can always tell good breeding—"

"He was a year or two ahead of me. You're getting close though."

"Of course I am. How about Nathan Pillsbury? He was in your class, wasn't he?"

"That's right."

"See!" she exclaimed triumphantly.

"He was in my class, all right. He was the teacher's pet, you might say." Raybe observed her over the rim of his bitter cup of tea.

"Nathan, my pet? Nathan Pillsbury? I don't remember any such thing. Besides, I never played favorites. That's a bad practice." She worked her lips to and fro.

"So's rapping people's knuckles." He laughed, putting his half-full cup on the floor.

She laughed her scattered little laugh again. "Oh, come now, Raybe. Surely it was deserved, if indeed I ever *did* rap your knuckles."

"You rapped them, all right," he said soberly.

"Did I? Did I really? Yes, I suppose I did. What was it for, do you remember? Passing notes? Gawking out the window?"

"It wasn't for any one thing. You did it lots of times. Dozens of times." He cleared his throat.

"Did I? Mercy me. It doesn't seem to me that I did. I only rapped knuckles upon extreme provocation, you know. Extreme provocation." She took a healthy swallow of tea to dismiss the matter.

"You did it lots of times," he continued. "In front of the whole class. They laughed at me." He made no effort to pick up his teacup again.

"I did? Goodness, what a memory! Well, it doesn't seem to have done you any harm. A little discipline never hurt anybody. What was it you said you've been doing professionally?"

"I've been in prison," he said with a pale smile. He watched her mouth draw downward in disapproval.

"Prison? You've been in prison? Oh, I see, it's a little joke." She tried to laugh again, but the little outburst wouldn't scatter this time.

"You try staying behind those walls for ten years and see if it's a joke." He fumbled in his pocket for a package of cigarettes, withdrew one, and slowly lit it. He blew the smoke across the table.

"Well, I must say! You're probably the only boy I ever had that . . . that ended up in prison! I'm sure there were . . . circumstances . . . leading up to that. I'm sure you're a fine lad, through it all." She worked her lips together faster now, and her gaze traveled to the window that looked out upon the black of night.

"Yeah, there were circumstances, as you call it. Very special circumstances." He blew an enormous smoke ring her way.

The old woman began to cough. "It's the smoke. I'm not used to people smoking around me. Do you mind refraining?"

"Yeah, I do mind," he said roughly. "I'm going to finish this cigarette, no matter what."

"Well, if you must, you must," she said nervously, half rising in her chair. "But let me just open that window a little—"

"Sit back down in that chair!" he ordered.

She fell back into the rocker like a bundle of rags.

"Now, you listen to me, you old bitch," he began.

"Don't you call me names. Don't you dare. How dare you? No wonder you were behind bars. A common jailbird. No respect for your elders."

"Shut up, Grandma." He tossed the cigarette butt to the floor and ground it out on the rug beneath his feet. Her eyes bulged as if they would pop.

"I remember you very clearly now," she exclaimed, her hands to her brow. "I remember you! You were no good to start with. A troublemaker. Always making trouble. I knew just where you'd end up. You've run true to form." Her gaze was defiant.

"Shut your mouth, Grandma," he said quietly, beginning to unzip his jacket at last.

"I will not, I'll have my say. I remember the day you wrote

nasty words on the wall in the supply closet. Horrible words. And then when I went back to get paper to distribute, I saw those words. I knew who wrote them, all right."

"I didn't write them."

"You wrote them, all right. And I whacked your knuckles good with a ruler, if I remember right."

"You whacked my knuckles good, but I didn't write the words."

"Did!"

"Didn't!" He squirmed out of the jacket.

"I never made mistakes of that kind," she said softly, watching him shed the jacket. "I knew just who needed strict discipline in my class."

He stood before her now, holding the heavy jacket in his hand. Underneath he wore only a tee shirt of some rough gray linsey-woolsey material. She was positive she could smell the odor of the prison upon him.

"I never made mistakes," she repeated feebly. "And now you'd better put that coat right back on and leave. Go back to where you came from."

"Can't do that just yet, Grandma. I got a score to settle."

"Score? To settle?" She placed her hands upon the rocker arms for support.

"Yeah. You're the one. You're the one that sent me to prison. I had a long time to figure it all out, see? Ten years to figure it out. Lots of nights I'd lie there on that hard old board of a bed in that puke-hole and I'd try to piece it all together. How I come to be there. Was it my aunt? Naw. She did the best she could without any money. Was it the fellas I took up with in high school? Naw, something happened before that, or I'd of never taken up with the likes of them. And then one night it came to me. *You* was the one."

"The one? The one for what?" Her lips worked furiously in and out like a bellows. Her hands tightly gripped the spindle arms of the rocker.

"The one that sent me there. Because you *picked* on me all the time. Made me out worse than I was. You never gave me the chance the others had. The other kids left me out of things because you were always saying I was bad. And you always told me I was dirty, just because my aunt couldn't keep me in clean shirts. You punished me for everything that happened. You even made fun of my name one day, and at recess all the boys called me "Raybe-Baby" and the name stuck. But the worst was the day of the words on the wall. You hit me so hard my knuckles bled. My hands were sore as boils for a week."

"That's an exaggeration."

"No it isn't. They're *my* hands, I ought to know! And do you know who wrote those words on the closet wall? *Do you know?*" he screamed, putting his face right down next to hers.

"No. Who?" she managed, breathless with fright.

"Nathan Pillsbury, that's who!" he shouted, clenching his teeth and shaking her frail body within his grasp. "Nathan Pillsbury! Nathan Pillsbury! *Nathan Pillsbury!*"

"Let me go," she whimpered into her sunken chest. "Let me go!"

"I'll let you go after my score is settled."

The old woman's eyes rolled upward toward the blank, unseeing windows. "What are you going to do to me?"

"Just settle my score, lady," he said, taking the hammer from his jacket. "Now, put your hands on the table top."

"My hands? On the table top?" she whispered.

"On the table top," he repeated pedantically. "Like this." He made two fists and placed them squarely on the surface. *"Like that!"* he yelled, wrenching her quivering hands and forcing them to the table top. Then with his free hand, he raised the hammer.

The Quality
of Feeling

Not long ago in Manhattan, Mr. Wayland-Smith led Petunia down the graveled path toward their customary bench overlooking the playground. At this hour nearly all the benches were empty, but he always chose this one: the sight of children was increasingly a comfort in his advancing years. Not that he felt old. He simply preferred the presence of children to that of the neighborhood crones who sat around complaining of ailments and talking incessantly of the weather.

The boys were already at play, Mr. Wayland-Smith saw with satisfaction: three or four were bouncing a ball against the side of the building directly adjacent to the small park. He settled himself on the bench, undid Petunia's leash, and unfolded the *Daily News* in his lap. While he scanned the terrible headlines proclaiming war and robbery and famine, the innocent cries of children mingled on the morning breeze.

He had barely looked at the paper when Petunia began her backing-up routine. She backed until she was resting completely on his shoes. That was her signal she wanted to be scratched, and every morning he pretended to protest. When his wiry fingers began to scratch her back, she rolled her eyes and grunted like a pig.

A Boston terrier, Petunia had a fat piglike body and a blunt snoutish face that had suggested her name to Mr. Wayland-Smith years before, when, by selling his last share of stock, he had acquired her to keep him company after the death of his good wife. He was a man not ordinarily given to whimsy, but the squat little dog with her astonishingly pink skin showing through her short fur looked for all the world like a pig to Mr. Wayland-Smith. And since she was a bitch, he couldn't call her Porky, could he? So Petunia it was, from a cartoon he had seen once at one of the Saturday matinees he regularly attended since retirement. He had sat surrounded by school children and laughed as hard as any of them when Petunia Pig broke a vase on Porky's head. That was the best time of the week, sitting in the neighborhood theater on Saturday afternoons, sometimes not even watching the picture, just listening to the laughs and squirms and whispers of hundreds of children.

Now that his Petunia was older and fatter, she even made little snorts and grunts as she labored beside Mr. Wayland-Smith down the city streets toward the park. It was almost as if she were obliging her master by becoming all the more porcine. As Mr. Wayland-Smith leaned forward on the bench to scratch Petunia, he became aware of his own outspread legs. His thighs looked plump in their trousers, like two hams. For the first time he realized that he, too, was becoming piglike. He had always heard that masters come to resemble their dogs, and he supposed there must be something to it after all. But the plumpness of his legs was where any resemblance ended. Petunia was not old, for a dog, not nearly as old as Mr. Wayland-Smith's corresponding years. Yet she seemed positively decrepit compared to him. He always walked with a spring in his step and his motions were quick and sure. Petunia waddled beside him like a little old lady. Everyone said Mr. Wayland-Smith was remarkable for his age. That was what Mr. Benjamin, the apartment-house manager, kept calling him: *remarkable*. Sitting in the park, Mr. Wayland-Smith rolled the word around in his mind, savoring it. *You are as old as you feel—* that was another saying he had heard all his life, and now he knew what it meant. He felt as young as one of those boys over there playing ball. Well, almost.

Mr. Wayland-Smith turned to the horoscope in the paper, which he always read assiduously. AVOID GOING OUT THIS MORNING, he read today. RESERVE ALL SOCIAL CONTACTS FOR THE AFTERNOON. Well, now he thought. What can that possibly mean? Why shouldn't he sit in the park as always? He fretted for a few moments over the horoscope. But he never had been able to take them all that seriously. Forty years as a public accountant had taught him that only figures can tell the truth, and sometimes even they lied.

Petunia rolled over on her back and studied Mr. Wayland-Smith with a positive grin on her face. She had so many facial expressions, she seemed quite human. He gave her a few pats and she closed her eyes. Soon he was feeling sleepy too. He leaned back on the slat bench and gave himself up to a nap. As he nodded off, the voices of the boys at play mingled with the sounds of traffic and a jackhammer somewhere in the distance. His last thought before sleep was to conjecture once more why the good Lord had deprived him of children. He and Cora had seen doctor after doctor—some of them expensive doctors he could not afford—and still they could never have any.

He was awakened by the gentlest of taps on the forehead. It might have been the warm brush of an angel's wing. Mr. Wayland-Smith's eyes snapped open like a sprung windowshade. For a moment everything was red. Then he saw it was a balloon. Some child's red balloon had drifted over to him in the morning breeze and bobbed against his head. He reached up for it and captured it between both hands. It must have been full of helium. Mr. Wayland-Smith regarded it with some humor, a bright and buoyant child's thing looking alien in his liver-spotted hands.

He had scarcely held the balloon a minute, turning his head this way and that looking for its owner, when three boys came scuffling down the gravel walk toward his bench. Two of them were older—about eleven or twelve, he would reckon—though he had little actual experience in guessing children's ages. The third boy was a little towhead no more than five. His eyes seemed saucer big, and they came to rest immediately on the balloon in Mr. Wayland-Smith's lap.

"Mine!" the young master cried in a delightfully hoarse voice. Was his voice always so hoarse, Mr. Wayland-Smith wondered? Perhaps the boy had recently had his tonsils removed. He understood that was something that frequently happened to young children. "Give it to me, it's mine," the boy continued.

"Oh, is it now?" Mr. Wayland-Smith asked with mock seriousness. He bugged his eyes the way he had seen some old men do, an expression that was foreign to him but seemed to fit the occasion. "How can I be sure? Do you have any proof?" He winked at the two older boys, involving them in his good-natured plot. But they did not respond. They stood stiff as stone and scowled into the sun.

"Give him back his balloon, mister," the taller one said. He was a much-freckled boy with plump cheeks and a tiny mouth. Mr. Wayland-Smith had never seen such a tiny mouth on a boy before; it might have been a slit in the top of a piggy bank.

"Well, now, I reckon I will, as soon as I determine it's his," Mr. Wayland-Smith said, continuing the persiflage. He noticed there was some black printing on the balloon, some words stamped there. "Did you put any marks on it, boy, to show that it's yours?" Again Mr. Wayland-Smith winked at the older boys, who glowered back. He looked at Petunia then, but she was still napping, her ears twitching in agitation at a fly that circled her head.

The freckled boy took two steps toward the bench. His fists were clenched. "You better give it to him, you old bastard, if you know what's good for you."

Mr. Wayland-Smith's jaw dropped open in surprise. What was this? What kind of language was this, coming from a boy to one of his elders? The boy wasn't even culturally deprived; he was well dressed, obviously from one of the apartment houses somewhere on the East side. Mr. Wayland-Smith held the balloon more firmly.

"You give Brucie his balloon, you dirty old bastard!" Freckle-face shouted. He lunged toward the old man and the balloon. Mr. Wayland-Smith raised the balloon high over his head. He tightened his fingers around it while the boy continued to scream words at him, words Mr. Wayland-Smith had never heard come from a boy before. Could he have been wrong about boys? Maybe he was wrong about children altogether. He clutched the balloon and when the freckle-faced boy pushed his head at him—breathing his hot sour breath directly into Mr. Wayland-Smith's face and calling him obscene names—his fingers tightened and tightened. Still the balloon would not burst. Finally he pressed both hands together as hard as he could and then it exploded, making a sound that nearly lifted him from the bench. Petunia jumped up, startled, and little shreds of rubber flew in all directions. One piece landed on his knee, a formless flaccid strip of red, wrinkled like an old grape.

As soon as the balloon burst, he was overcome with an enormous feeling of relief. *I did it and I'm glad!* he thought to himself. *That's a most wretched little boy.* Then Brucie began to cry, and Mr. Wayland-Smith was heavily repentant. After all, it was not Brucie's fault his older brother—or whoever

Freckle-face was—was such a monster. Brucie howled and Petunia circled his feet, perplexed. Brucie's fair face was turning nearly as red as the late-lamented balloon.

Mr. Wayland-Smith hawked his throat, stalling for time, trying to think of something to say by way of apology for his extraordinary act.

"Old bastard!" Freckle-face said. "Dirty old bastard." His little slit of a mouth snapped open and closed like a change purse.

The other older boy, with curly black hair and an oily forehead that glistened in the light, joined in. "Yeah, you dirty old bastard. What'd you do it for, huh?" His words fell leaden; it was obvious he hadn't an original thought in his head. Probably all his short life he had been echoing the words of Freckle-face.

Mr. Wayland-Smith sat tall on his bench. He would not be talked to this way by mere striplings. "It was unintentional, I assure you. An accident. The whole thing was an accident, and I'll ask you to keep a civil tongue in your heads."

"Accident, my foot!" Freckle-face said, getting quite heated. "We saw it all, didn't we, Ernie?"

"Yeah," the greasy one said. "We saw it all." He spat on the gravel.

"We saw you. You grabbed up his balloon and held on to it and weren't going to give it back, ever."

"I was. Of course I was," Mr. Wayland-Smith protested, feeling victimized. Surely this dreadful boy was going too far.

"No, you weren't, you old bastard. You weren't never going to give it back. And when I tried to get it away from you—you busted it on purpose!"

"Yeah," Ernie said and spat again.

Brucie continued to cry louder and turn redder.

Petunia rolled her milky eyes and interjected low howls to add to the clamor.

"Honestly," Mr. Wayland-Smith mumbled, casting his head

about in embarrassment, looking to see if any adults had observed his folly. But the small park was empty except for the four of them. Finally he plunged his hand in his pants pocket and discovered three coins, three quarters. "Look," he said, rubbing the coins together in his fingers. "I'll pay the boy for his balloon. How's that? I'll be glad to pay for it. How much? How much did it cost? I'll give him money for another."

"Can't replace that balloon," Freckle-face said truculently. "It was his souvenir from the World's Fair. It even had 'World's Fair' written right on the side of it."

"Well, can't you take him out to the Fair and get him another one?" Mr. Wayland-Smith asked in exasperation. He was more than ready to vacate his bench, to return to the sanctuary of his apartment across the street.

"Stupid! Don't you know anything? The Fair closed down last Saturday! Everything's boarded up or knocked down."

"Well, buy him some other kind of balloon, then. This *is* New York City. You can get all sorts of balloons. Here, take it—" In a moment of dazzling generosity, he thrust all three quarters at the boy. It was more than he supposed any balloon cost, even a World's Fair balloon. He should have given them just one or two of the quarters at most. But he was in no position to stint. He had deliberately destroyed Brucie's balloon. But at seventy-five cents it had been an expensive revenge; he would have to economize all this week to make up for it. There were two more weeks before his next Social Security check arrived. How would he do it? Skip buying the paper seven mornings in a row. Give up his Saturday matinee. Something like that. He didn't feel much like a Saturday matinee now anyhow. He could economize on breakfasts too. Every other morning he had eggs and canned corned-beef hash; alternate mornings he ate just instant oatmeal and tea. Perhaps he would have oatmeal seven consecutive mornings this week: oatmeal cost next to nothing, you make it with water. Certainly he would not consider cutting down on Petunia's food.

Freckle-face pocketed the money without a word and moved away from the bench. As soon as he was a safe distance, he shook his fist at Mr. Wayland-Smith and yelled, "You old bastard! You busted Brucie's balloon on purpose! We'll get you!"

"Yeah, you old bastard, we'll get you," the greasy one echoed.

"Keep quiet, just keep quiet!" Mr. Wayland-Smith said with surprising vehemence. By gum, it was worth all of seventy-five cents to break the little bastard's balloon, just to teach them a lesson, he thought. Then he recoiled at his own thought and stood up. He clipped the leash to Petunia's collar and, as soon as the boys were out of the park and around the corner, he crunched down the gravel toward home.

The next morning Mr. Wayland-Smith was back in the park as usual. He had tried to put the unpleasant incident of the balloon out of mind, but that was impossible. After all, it had caused him to deprive himself of an egg and hash for breakfast. It had caused him to hurry by the newsstand in the lobby like a pauper, carefully avoiding the eye of Freddie, the man who sold him a *Daily News* every morning. Freddie would wonder why he didn't stop for his copy this morning—tomorrow morning too, for that matter. But Mr. Wayland-Smith was determined to adjust his budget to accommodate the seventy-five cents he literally had thrown to the wind.

As Mr. Wayland-Smith and Petunia entered the park, the old man saw that the playground was deserted. Usually some boys played ball beyond the flower beds, perhaps the same three boys he had encountered, he could not recall: while it had always been pleasant to have children about, he had never memorized their faces. Children had always been just children, happy, neuter, anonymous. Today he was relieved to see there was no one else in the park but a colored nanny with a smart navy-blue baby carriage. If there had been boys here—the boys with whom he had had the altercation—he probably would not have entered the park at all. But where was there to go? He could not spend all morning on a stool in Walgreen's drugstore, nursing a single cup of tea. And the thought of spending all day in his room made him singularly claustrophobic.

Because he had no paper to read in the park, Mr. Wayland-Smith petted Petunia more elaborately than usual. He freed her of her leash and she rolled on her back and wriggled like a pig in clover. He played with her until the warmth of the soporific sun seeped into his bones. Then he rested his freshly shaved chin on his chest and napped. Petunia curled about his feet to take her ease. She was a great comfort, Petunia was.

When he awoke he could feel she no longer was on his shoes. Apprehension rose in his chest like nausea. Then he saw her, just a few yards away, playing with some children. He thought that unusual; normally she never left his side. He squinted into the sun and as his eyes adjusted he saw the same three boys. He rose stiffly from his bench then and took a few steps toward them. "Petunia? Here girl. Here Petunia."

The boys turned toward him and smiled. Their smiles were dazzling in the high morning sun. Freckle-face waved to him. "She's all right, mister. We're just playing."

"Yeah. We're just playing," greasy Ernie said with a giggle.

Little Brucie patted Petunia on top of her head, and the fat terrier shamelessly switched her stub of a tail and roguishly rolled her eyes.

"She's not used to children," Mr. Wayland-Smith explained, walking toward the group. "Petunia?"

The dog didn't turn to look at him at all.

"She's all right, honest," Freckle-face said.

"Nice doggie," Brucie crowed in his hoarse voice.

"Petunia, come here. I mean it," Mr. Wayland-Smith commanded.

"Over here, girl," Freckle-face coaxed. "Over here. Nice girl—" He ran down the park and Petunia followed him, her belly rolling from side to side like the wattles on a turkey.

"Petunia! Come back!" Mr. Wayland-Smith cried. But the dog ran on and on, across the world on the grass, never looking back at him. "Petunia!" he called, but soon she was just a wagging black dot on the horizon. Why should she go off with those boys? he wondered in bafflement. She had never run off with anyone before. Did she long to run and play? Had she secretly been feeling pent up and restricted living with him? Maybe Petunia had only been tolerating him all these years. "Petunia!" he cried out in terror, his voice sounding strangled in his throat.

"She's all right!" Freckle-face yelled to him. "We'll take good care of her!"

Mr. Wayland-Smith tried to run, but his old legs wouldn't carry him far. He stopped in the dewy grass, whispering Petunia's name, while the dog and the boys passed through the iron gates at the far end of the park and were gone.

"Them boys sure like your little doggie," the Negro nanny said, wheeling the blue baby carriage past him. "I call that real nice, you letting them play with her like that."

He wanted to ask her to help him, but what could she do? What could anybody do? They were just three boys with no names, three boys who might be brothers or who might not be, three boys who could live anywhere in New York City or beyond. When he finally reached the gate, they were nowhere in sight.

Mr. Wayland-Smith sank to a bench just inside the gate, an isolated bench he had never sat on before, and waited for a long time. He waited until late afternoon, though he had known, the minute Petunia passed through that gate, he would never see her again. He waited because it was the thing to do, the only thing he could do, and finally he left the bench, feeling as if he were asleep. He didn't even return to the bench near the playground for the empty collar and leash. His face was white and drawn, with little splotches of red on each cheek. As he passed the newsstand, Freddie remarked to himself that Mr.

Wayland-Smith was getting along in years. He had never noticed before how much the old boy was showing his age. Just now he had passed with a decided stoop to his shoulders, a shuffle in his step.

That night Mr. Wayland-Smith had a dream: He dreamed he was eating steak and French fries and ice cream, when the buzzer sounded at his door. He rushed to the door and unbolted it. No one was standing there. Then he looked down and saw her: Petunia was lying on the Welcome mat, her dead eyes staring up at him like two agate marbles. Her little limbs were distended stiff as stobs. Her little teeth showed and her beautiful pink and black gums were drawn in a grimace of pain. Her belly had been ripped open from chin to groin, and even now gray and pink intestines spilled out slowly all over his floor.

For a moment Mr. Wayland-Smith had to cling to the door frame for support. Then he stooped to scoop her in his arms. As he knelt there he was certain he heard the sound of children's laughter echoing down the hallway.